THE ORPHAN PICKPOCKET'S CHRISTMAS

VICTORIAN ROMANCE

JESSICA WEIR

PUREREAD.COM

CONTENTS

DEAR READER, GET READY FOR ANOTHER GREAT STORY...

A VICTORIAN ROMANCE

I n the heart of 1875 Victorian London, where the city's ruthless streets guard the darkest of secrets, two orphaned souls stand defiant in the face of adversity....

Turn the page and let's begin

CHAPTER 1

E mma Mason walked along the street and stared at the beautiful dresses of the women who bustled around the market. They were like proud peacocks, displaying their feathers for all the world to see. It made Emma sad. Once she had worn beautiful dresses, or at least nice dresses, but that was before Papa left. He had been gone for over six years now and things were getting slowly worse. The dress she wore was worn in places and had been extended with a hem of contrasting material to keep up with her growth. She would soon be sixteen and hoped that her mama would allow her to get a new gown.

As she had the thought, they passed a milliner's shop. In the window was the most delightful bonnet. It was light blue with pink edging. The blue lace was weaved through with pink ribbon. For a moment Emma imagined what it would feel like to wear it. Of course, with a matching dress. She would hold her head high and walk down the street smiling at every handsome boy who gave her a wink.

Of course, Mama would never let her have such a beautiful hat, never mind a dress that would go with it, but she could dream. As always, when she dreamed of something better, she thought of their papa.

"When is Papa coming home?" she asked her mother who walked along at her side hauling the basket with the goods from the market.

Pamela Mason sighed. "How many times have I told you child, that I don't want to talk about it?"

"But, Mama, I only have my memories and they are fading. Will you tell me a little about him?" Emma had hoped that her mother would soften one day. She had asked this same question, or others like it a thousand times and it either made her mother angry or withdrawn. Emma thought that she was probably sad but that she didn't want to admit it. That was why she snapped and changed the subject.

"Watch where you're walking," Pamela said.

Emma held her foot in mid-air, just in time to avoid a rather nasty looking puddle. Runoff from the butchers had congealed into a horrid mess that was buzzing with flies and would have stained the hem of her dress. Stepping over, Emma wondered if she should try again.

She was feeling bold as she had seen the small rabbit that her mama had haggled for in the market. They would have meat in their stew tonight.

"When will he be back?" Emma asked.

Another sigh. "Benedict is gone, let's just leave it that way."

"Did he abandon us, Mama?" Emma always felt hurt. It was as if her mother was trying to protect her and her memories of her papa. It always made her wonder if he had run off with someone else. Had he found someone prettier than her mama and her? Did he get tired of her brother David's crying? The boy was nine now but he was still young when Papa left. Why would he abandon them? They used to have a nice house. Now they lived in two rooms of a tenement, in a slum close to the Old Nicol. Surely, he loved them too much to leave them to this?

"Stop asking questions. Your papa loved you and he had to go away. You know that is all I will say on this."

"But, Mama, if he loved us…"

The sound of a scuffle broke out followed by shouting.

"Thief, thief, stop that boy."

The sound of the Peelers' whistles echoed around the market place followed by running footsteps that rumbled across the cobblestones.

Emma peered through the crowds trying to get a better look. A young boy, he looked about Emma's age perhaps a little older, had tried to take a gold pocket watch. The fine gentleman had pushed him over and shouted *thief*. Only, the boy was quick and got to his feet weaving in and out of the crowds as the larger but more ungainly police tried to catch him. He passed by Emma and her mother, and Emma and he locked eyes. It only lasted for a split second, but it felt a lot longer. He had such a look of shame on his face, and his eyes seemed to beg forgiveness from her. As soon as he had come, he was gone, scampering off into the crowd and to freedom.

"You must never steal," Pamela said in her most stern voice. It was her second rule, the first being that no one should ask about their father. "Bad things happen to thieves. They go to the gallows or are taken away. Never steal, no matter how bad it gets. Do you hear me, girl?"

Emma pulled her eyes away from the crowd. This time the boy had escaped. A vision of his dirty cheeks and the mud caked knees that showed below his trousers came to her mind. Why would he do such a thing?

"Come now, girl, let's get home and prepare this lovely rabbit," Pamela said.

Emma smiled and wondered how long it would last them. Her stomach rumbled as she realized it had been over a week since they had eaten any meat. For now, she put the thoughts of her father behind her and wondered how she could help them now. Maybe she could get a job. Mama worked in service at a big house just an hour's walk away from their home. Perhaps they would take her on. Across the market she saw a handsome man selling veg. Then there was her favourite dream. Perhaps she would find a rich and handsome man to marry her and all their problems would be over.

"Stop dawdling, girl," Pamela said. "I want to get home to remind your brother what happens to thieves."

Soon, they were walking down dirtier, and smellier streets. Emma only noticed the smell when she came back into the slum that was now her home. It was the smell of outhouses and dead cats. Of discarded rubbish and decay, but you soon got used to it. A rat ran along the building before them. For a moment, it stopped and turned to look back. Its beady black eyes stared like death and Emma shuddered. She had once heard a story that rats would come for you at night and nibble out your eyes. With a flick of its tail it was gone, disappearing into a shrub that grew out of the corner of a house.

"Stop dawdling, girl, I have to pay the rent today."

Emma realized that her mama was still walking and now that the rat had gone, she ran to catch up. Only, another shudder went down her spine. Paying the rent always made Mama anxious. It was rare that they would have meat on rent day... still, the rabbit had been pretty mangled and not too fresh. But it wasn't her mama's anxiety that made her uneasy. What caused this feeling was Jairus Cuthbert. Emma wasn't sure if he owned the building that they and four other families lived in, or if he merely collected the rent. Either way she dreaded seeing him.

As they arrived back at the house, she was hoping to avoid Jairus but that wouldn't happen. The man was leaning against the wall of their building. A pipe in his mouth, one hand on his prominent gut. As they drew nearer, he reached for his pocket watch and shook his head. Mama increased the speed of her walking whilst Emma hung back, hoping to remain unnoticed in her mother's shadow.

It wasn't to be. The landlord licked his slug like lips and his dark beady eyes reminded her of the rat. Running a hand through his slicked-back black hair, a smile came to those abhorrent lips.

"Mrs Mason, I was beginning to think you were not going to pay today," he said, keeping his eyes on Emma.

"I'm sorry, Mr Cuthbert, Emma here has been dawdling today. You know how children have their head in the clouds sometimes," Pamela passed Emma the basket whilst she rummaged in her coin purse.

"That one's no longer a child," Jairus said. "If you struggle with the rent, well, I'm sure we can come to some arrangement. I'm looking for a new wife, since the last one passed on."

"Mr. Cuthbert!"

"Here," Pamela said as she handed over the coins. "That will happen over my dead body."

"Be careful what you wish for." Cuthbert grinned and then stepped aside to let them pass.

Back in their two rooms they found David playing with his wooden train. It was worn now, the paint all rubbed away. It was the last present their father had carved for him before he disappeared and David treasured it like nothing else.

Emma went to sit with her brother for a few minutes. This morning she had scoured the neighbourhood with him for wood. They had found enough scraps to light a small fire. Hopefully, it would be enough to cook the rabbit. Only, Mama was not preparing the meal. Instead, she had removed the loose floorboard in the corner of the room and was counting their coins. There was something about her face that worried Emma.

"What is it, Mama?"

Pamela looked up and shook her head. "It's nothing, child. Help me prepare this rabbit. I have a few carrots and a turnip; we will have us a hearty stew for a few nights. Along with the bread, we will feast like the queen."

Emma felt a flush of joy go through her. What would it be like to feast like the queen? She ruffled David's mop of curly blond hair and left the boy to play while she prepared the vegetables. All the time she dreamed of the handsome man she would marry. How he would buy her fine dresses. They would live in a house with a bath and would eat meat every day. There would be coal to put on the fire and a clean blanket. It put a smile on her face and drove out the chill left by Jairus from earlier.

With the fire lit, and the stew pot hung over it, the rooms were soon filled with a delicious smell. Emma sat on the pallet she shared at night with her mama while David played with his train. Emma wanted to keep dreaming but she knew something was wrong.

"Mama, I was wondering…"

"Yes, child?"

"Maybe I could work with you at the big house… maybe that would make you happier?"

Pamela left the stew and came over to sit down next to her. "I'm not unhappy, child."

"Something is wrong," Emma said, feeling more and more certain that she was right.

"We are just a little short of coin. It is nothing to worry about and you need to look after your brother most days."

"I can manage on my own," David said looking up with the face of an angel and big blue eyes that convinced you he was one.

"I know you can," Pamela said. For a few moments she was quiet and she seemed to be staring at nothing. Her fingers twiddled the wedding band that she still wore. It was a habit she had and Emma doubted she even knew she was doing it.

"I will talk to the housekeeper," Pamela said at last. "If they agree, we will start you on two days a week first and build you up, how does that sound?"

"It sounds great," Emma said. Part of her really wanted to do this. Knew that she was old enough to take some of the burden off her sweet mama, and yet she felt worried that her world was about to change. In her experience, change was never good.

CHAPTER 2

It had been two weeks since Emma started working at the big house. The walk there and back took an hour each way and the first time she had loved it. As they gradually came out of the slums the sights, sounds, and smells were even better than the markets. The ladies wore such colourful dresses, the men in their jackets, breeches and top hats were a sight to be seen. So handsome that she wanted to swoon. The girlish part of her wanted one of these men to notice her. To see through her patched dress, and just a few weeks ago, that would be all that was on her mind. Only, she reckoned that she was growing up for a part of her knew that was just childish. Men didn't rescue pretty maidens, not even their fathers.

Then there was the smell, perfume drifted on the air, from the ladies and from flowers that grew in the gardens of the houses. The air was breathable and clean, fresh almost.

The smell of newly cooked bread seemed to fill the air and make her stomach rumble and her mouth salivate.

Horses and carriages of all shapes and sizes were everywhere. The sound of their hooves clip-clopping down the street as the carriage wheels rumbled along behind.

It was like going into a different world, only at night, when she was exhausted, she had to make the long walk home. This time the world gradually got dimmer. The light and bright streets with their now sweet smells of cooking meat and roasting vegetables were replaced with the smell of sewer and things long rotten. On that first walk home she had come to understand her position in life and to realise that it was not good. Once more she had wanted to ask about her papa but it seemed childish and she could see a fatigue in her mother that worried her. As they walked home in silence, she understood that one day her mother would be gone and she wanted to drop down in the dirty street and cry.

That had been two weeks ago and in this short time she had become accustomed to the long hours and hard work. Already she understood the burden her mother had carried and yet Pamela never moaned or mentioned it. In her mind, it just was.

They were halfway through the walk back and Emma could still feel her hands stinging. Monday was wash day. As the new girl she had been given this task. It meant hours of dunking her hands into scalding water and scrubbing until her fingers were raw.

Several times during the day she had seen her mother hovering nearby. It was obvious that she wanted to take over, but that she was resisting. Each time, Emma had thrown her one of her most dazzling smiles. Though she wanted the help, she was determined to do her bit.

The housekeeper's name was Martha Jones, she was a big woman with rosy red cheeks and a face that you expected to smile. It didn't, or at least, not that Emma had seen. Somehow, she didn't think that the woman would like it if her mother helped her. In fact, she wondered if she might even get her mother in trouble. The woman had a temper and didn't mind raising her voice to issue an order. Whenever she did maids, cooks, sculleries, and footmen all ducked their heads and buckled down to work.

All afternoon, the woman had been watching as Emma folded the washed item and brought it all back to the kitchen. It was someone else's job to iron it, which was a big relief. The ever-watching housekeeper made her nervous. So much so, that she was afraid that she might burn something if she was left to use the flat iron. It was a tool she had hardly ever used but she had watched her mother. First, you had to heat it on the stove and then with a cloth, you carefully ironed the clothes. Only, it was a job that required a lot of skill and caution. Otherwise, the beautiful linens and clothing would be ruined.

Emma pushed the thought of the work behind her. It was harder than she expected. In her mind she had imagined making lots of new friends. As it was, she had hardly had time to mutter more than a *hello* to the equally busy maids and scullions. The handsome footmen in their uniforms of black jackets with the shiny buttons had hardly cast her a glance. At first, she thought that they thought her beneath them, but she now realized that they were too busy doing their own jobs to notice one more maid. At least, she too had a uniform just like her mama's. The black dress with the heavily starched white apron was the nicest thing she had worn in many years. Even the bonnet made her feel good as she walked down the street.

Tomorrow she was to work in the kitchen. Preparing the potatoes and washing pots as well as scrubbing the floor and general cleaning. Maybe then she would have more time to get to know her new workmates.

"You're very quiet," her mother said as they walked past the now closed market.

"Sorry, I was thinking."

"If it's too much for you, we can try to find you something easier," Pamela added.

"No, Mama, it's not that." Emma wanted to stop the work, but she was beginning to understand that they needed the money. She was also beginning to understand the looks that Jairus gave her and what they meant. She was even beginning to understand that they could end up worse than they were. Going to the big house with all its luxuries had not made her feel worse about her current situation. It had, in fact, made her realise just how lucky she was. For each morning and night as they walked the long road to and from work, she saw the poor. People sleeping in corners and begging for bread. How could she not have seen it before? "I like the job... I'm just a little tired is all." Emma had found the lie came easily to her lips but she could see that her mother believed none of it.

"I think I will talk to Mrs Jones, see if I can get you an easier position," Pamela said.

Emma nearly shouted *no*; she remembered Mrs Jones telling her that this was not a free ride. Before she got the easy jobs, she had to pay her dues. Somehow, she didn't think the steely old woman would take kindly to her mother asking for favours. So how could she distract her? It came to her right away. What always stopped her mother talking?

"When will you tell me more about Papa?" Emma said in a slightly more childish voice. One that was bound to annoy her mother.

"There is nothing to tell. He isn't here and you must remember that he's not coming back."

"Why?" Emma was angry now, maybe because she was tired.

"Because I said so. Now hurry along, David has been alone too long."

With that her mother put her head down, pulled her shawl tighter around her shoulders and increased her stride. She was almost running down the cobblestone street, but what was she running from?

Things carried on just as normal for the next two weeks. Emma became more used to the punishing work and her mother still refused to tell her about her father. They were visiting the market and Emma found her eyes drawn to all the sights and sounds. Things seemed different now for she was an adult, working, she even had a coin in her pocket that her mother had said she could spend how she liked.

She had yet to decide if to get some apples, bread, or a piece of ribbon for her hair. One good thing about the job was that they got a meal after the household had eaten. It was often only bread and butter but it eased the burden on the family purse just a little more. How could she not have noticed how much her mother was struggling?

As her eyes flitted about the market, she watched David running along ahead of them. He was doing fine and had even asked if he could buy some flowers to sell. He had seen another boy doing this, but Mama had said *no*. For now, he ran around the market, his train ever in his hands.

Then she saw the coffee stall and looked up at her mama. Pamela understood and she nodded. They would all have a treat. For only 1d they would get a small cup of coffee and two *thin*, that was two thin slices of bread and butter.

Soon they were sitting on a wall at the edge of the market enjoying their treat. The bread was fresh and warm and tasted better than anything she'd had in a long time. She knew that this was only because it was such a treat. One they had not been able to enjoy for many years. Perhaps, David never had. His train was on his lap as he tucked into the bread, a big grin on his chubby little cheeks.

"Thank you, Emma," he managed through a mouthful of food.

"Manners, young man," Pamela said but there was nothing but joy in her voice. She was happy. They sat on the wall and ate and drank for quite some time. Emma stared around the market and imagined that she saw a handsome fruit and vegetable seller looking her way and smiling. He was tall and lean and had blond hair that must have once been a little like David's. Had he smiled at her?

Before she could decide Pamela started to cough. Emma turned to her mother as another cough racked her body. Pamela stopped and pulled out a handkerchief. Gently she mopped her brow and shook her head.

"Are you all right, Mama?" Emma asked.

"It's nothing, just a summer cold."

Emma nodded and yet she couldn't take her eyes off her mother. There was a slight sheen to her brow and she had been coughing more and more recently. Though it was still summer it had rained heavily for over a week. Pamela had been caught in the rain several days on her long journey to work. Perhaps she had picked up something, perhaps she needed to rest.

Emma offered her mama the last drops of coffee and it seemed to ease the cough. For now, the handsome man had been forgotten.

CHAPTER 3

The following Monday as they walked back to the house after working Emma could see Jairus waiting at the door as he often did. The pipe was in his mouth spewing a horrid smelling smoke as always. One thing Emma had noticed was that her mother was no longer so worried about the rent. She knew her own pay was not much but it was helping and that thought brought a smile to her face.

Seeing the smile, Jairus's eyes widened and his tongue flicked out across his lips. "Emma, Mrs Mason, good day to you."

"Mr Cuthbert, I have your rent." Pamela was holding her coin purse in one hand and offered him the coin with the other. As she passed it over, her intention had been to walk right by him, but more nimbly than Emma expected, he stepped in front of the door and blocked their way.

"Thank you, Mrs Mason, but I was wondering if you would like to move into a nicer part of the house?"

"No, thank you, we are quite happy where we are."

There was something in his eyes that made Emma blush and want to run and hide. It was like he wanted to eat her up and spit out her bones, and it made her skin crawl.

"Well, in that case I wondered if you would mind if I call on Emma sometime? Just for a talk, so we can get to know each other a little better."

"I do mind! She is just a child and you will leave her alone. My husband will be returning soon and if he heard you say such a thing..." Pamela didn't finish the sentence but shoved past him leaving a gap for Emma to get through.

Emma ran after her mother, not sure whether she was more shocked at what had just happened. What had just happened? Why had it made her mama so mad when he asked to call on her? Or whether she was so shocked to hear that her papa was coming home. As they raced up the stairs to their room, she found her heart open its wings and soar to the moon. Was Papa really coming home? Would he take them back to their nice house? Would Mama be able to give up her job? It was all her greatest dreams come true.

As they opened the door to go into their rooms, Emma's mind was buzzing with questions. Which should she ask first? Before she could decide, David was there to greet them. He looked a little subdued but that didn't matter now. Nothing mattered but the fact that their papa was coming home.

"When?" was the only word Emma could manage as Pamela sat down on a chair by the small table.

Her mother looked up at her and there was moisture in the corner of her eyes. Before Emma could say anything, Pamela was racked with another bout of coughing. It hacked at her body. The sound was like something was breaking inside. Like each cough tore something loose. Emma dropped to her knees beside her mother and rubbed her back, trying anything to help, but the coughing wouldn't stop.

"David, is there any water?" Emma asked without even looking at the boy.

David nodded and went to the pitcher on the table. He was a good boy and often went to the pump to bring in water without being asked. Quickly he returned with a mug and handed it to her.

Emma assisted her mother to drink; it helped, and the coughing gradually subsided as Pamela took gentle sips. As she passed the cup back, Emma noticed that there was blood on the side and in the water. This could not be good.

Emma helped her mama onto the pallet that they shared and covered her with a blanket. By now she was shivering and yet there was a thin sheen of sweat soaking through her clothes and dripping off her skin.

They had a little stew left and had picked up some bits at the market. Leaving her mama to sleep, Emma went about preparing some supper.

"Is Mama all right?" David asked.

Emma looked down into his huge blue eyes. They were so innocent and so caring. She just wanted to pull him into her arms and tell him everything was going to be all right. That Papa was coming home soon and that he would take care of all of them. It had to be true. Her mother would not have said it if it wasn't true, would she? Only she couldn't tell him anything. If it wasn't true or didn't happen as quickly, as a young boy would expect, then he would be heartbroken.

"She will be fine, it's just a summer cold. Now, you play with your train while I make us some stew."

"I found some wood," he said as he went over to the corner where he played with that train for hours. It was a corner where there was a curtain over his own cot. The corner where he slept but he always seemed so happy there. For him there were no silly dreams of a girl who hoped for a handsome man to rescue her. For him there was just the train and his love for his family.

Emma handed her mother a bowl of stew and a hunk of bread and they sat together at the table as a family. All eating in silence. It was only after David had gone to bed that Emma dared bring up what was on her mind.

"How are you?" she asked first.

Her mother looked down at the table first and for one awful moment Emma thought that she would cough again. She didn't but as she looked up Emma thought that she had aged ten years in the last few days. Why had she not noticed it sooner?

"I'm all right," Pamela said, "but I know there is another question that has been burning your lips for some hours."

Emma felt tears in her own eyes. They were partly for her papa and partly for the worry that her mother was worse than she was saying. Surely, it could not be right that she was bleeding when she coughed?

"I will tell you about him child, but not tonight. My chest hurts as does my throat. Just know that he never left of his own accord. He had no choice at what he did... though, at times I hate him for it, it was necessary, and he did it for you and David."

Emma felt her mouth drop open. That was the most her mother had ever said about her father. Though it left her with more questions than answers, it filled her with a joy that could lift her up and carry her on its wings. Her papa had cared. He hadn't abandoned them and maybe, just maybe he would come home when he could.

Pamela started to cough again and Emma helped her to the pallet and tucked her into the bed.

That night Emma couldn't sleep even though she knew she had to get up to go to work early the next morning. All night she heard her mother cough on and off but there was nothing she could do. Sips of water didn't help. As the night wore on her mother was covered with sweat. Taking a damp washcloth, she did her best to cool her brow, but it was no good. This was bad and her heart ached as she wondered if she would lose her mother rather than gain a father.

CHAPTER 4

Morning came quicker than she expected. Emma had fallen asleep at her mother's side. It was the crow of a cockerel that woke her and she jerked up to see that it would soon be light. Lighting a candle she came to her mother's bedside.

"How are you?" she asked as Pamela's eyes opened.

"I'm fine." Her mother's voice was scratchy and Emma offered her a drink.

"Take a rest while I make breakfast," Emma said. Many times she had made the gruel but since she had been working her mother had taken over for her as a small treat. Today she went about the familiar routine of mixing the gruel and heating it.

All the time her mother coughed and coughed. Slowly she was trying to put on her clothes but she kept sinking to the floor. Emma felt her heart sink down so low it seemed to pull her shoulders with it. Would they lose their mother? No, she must not think that way. She must be strong.

"Go back to bed, Mama," Emma said. "I will let Mrs Jones know that you are too ill to work today."

"No, child," a coughing fit took Pamela before she could finish and she slumped back to the bed pallet, lying still for a few long moments.

Emma's hand had frozen over the pot of gruel and it was only when it began to burn that she pulled it away. "Mama!" she said as she rushed over to the bed. "Please, Mama do not leave us."

Emma dropped to her knees and with a shaking hand she reached out to touch her mother's shoulder. The pain in her heart was telling her it was too late. That her mother had gone. And she was afraid to touch her and confirm the truth.

Slowly, her hand reached out and as it held her mother's sweat-soaked shoulder, Pamela drew in another breath. Emma hugged her mother tight and pulled her close to hide her tears from David.

"Emma, Emma, what is wrong?" David asked from behind her.

Emma sat up and wiped the tears from her eyes before turning to look at David. "Mama is not too well. We need to be brave, and to take care of her."

David nodded, but she could see the tears shining in his big blue eyes and it broke her heart. Whatever happened, she must stay strong for him, but what could she do? Then it came to her, there was the apothecary on the corner of the market. She would go into work, explain what was happening, and then go to the apothecary. Surely, he would know how to save their mother.

David was still close to tears and Emma knew she had to do something. The slight scent of burning told her that the first thing was to tend to the breakfast. Moving over to the pot over the fire she stirred it delicately. Making sure not to scrape the bottom which was surely burnt.

"David, why don't you go pump some more water, while I finish breakfast?"

David's little face lit up. Having something to do had obviously helped him.

Stirring the gruel helped calm Emma. It was normal. It was every day. The routine of it eased her pain and helped her concentrate. There was much to do and she had to make sure that she kept David calm.

Within just a few minutes he returned with the pitcher of the fresh water. They were lucky, the well in the garden was deep and the water always seemed to be clean. Over the last few years, there had been rumours about people who got sick from their water. She did not know whether to believe it, but the water was all they had. Setting up three bowls of the gruel, she sat David at the table and was happy to see that he tucked into his breakfast hungrily. The little boy didn't understand how serious things were. Maybe it was best he stayed that way.

Leaving her own bowl near the hearth where it would stay warm, Emma took the third one over to her mother. Gently, she put her arm behind her mother's head. There was a flicker from Pamela's eyes but nothing more. At least she could see the steady rise and fall of her mother's chest. She was breathing, and it was easier now that this coughing had stopped. Emma wanted to get some food down her mother and was almost tempted to shake her awake, but the stress that could cause to David wasn't worth it. So she poured the gruel back into the pot and returned to the table with her own portion.

Putting on a brave smile, she ate her food, even though it tasted like sawdust in her mouth. The gruel was dry; even if it wasn't, she doubted she could eat it, but she forced herself to swallow and smiled again at David.

"Mama is going to stay here today, and you will be brave and look after her. What do you think of that?"

His blue eyes lit up for a moment but then they widened more and more until they seemed to fill his face. "I don't know how."

"All you need to do is bring her water when she asks for it and take a damp cloth and wipe her brow every now and then. Apart from that, you just need to be here for her. You can play with your train, just as you normally would. Mama will be happy knowing that you are here." She added on at the end: "And pray, please."

David smiled. It seemed that the simple instructions pleased him. "Maybe I will talk while I play, then she will know what I'm doing, and she might want to join in."

"I think she might, when she is a little better," Emma said. "I will walk to work and let them know what is happening and then I will go to the apothecary and bring some medicine. I am sure that Mama will be well again in no time."

David nodded and pushed away his bowl. "I need to go to the outhouse; can I play after?"

Emma reached over and ruffled his curly blond hair. "Of course, you can. I'm going to get off now so that I can get back as soon as I can. You be a good boy, you hear."

David giggled as he ran from the house. He would make his way out into the muddy garden and all the way across, past the well to the outhouse. It was used by everyone in the building, and at times could get quite unpleasant.

Their mother had always made sure that it was as clean as could be. Somehow, just that thought had fresh tears pushing at the back of her eyes. For the first time in a long while she prayed. Prayed to the Lord that her mother would be saved. She had the feeling this would not be the last time she would pray in earnest.

Emma couldn't manage the rest of her breakfast. Both hers and her mothers were poured back into the pot. It would be there for tomorrow.

Quickly, she checked on her mother again. Wiping Pamela's sweat-drenched brow, she leaned down and whispered into her ear, "I love you, Mama, and I will be back soon."

Placing a quick kiss on her forehead she turned to leave, for she knew if she didn't go soon, she never would. Grabbing her shawl, she rushed out of the house. The journey to work normally took them an hour. This morning she trotted along the dirty streets and onto the cobblestone street and on and on until her own breath was catching in her throat and her lungs were bursting.

She arrived at the big house in around forty minutes. As she rushed into the kitchen one of the maids stepped back, a look of shock on her face.

"You can't let Mrs. Jones see you like that," Mary said.

"What, why?" Emma asked only she already understood. The race to get here had meant she had lost her bonnet and her hair was soaked with sweat and dishevelled. No doubt her uniform was as bad. "My mama is dreadfully sick, I need to take her some medicine, do you think she will let me?" Emma pleaded as she fought to regain her breath.

"She won't be pleased about it," Mary said as she grabbed a fresh bonnet from a pile of clothing and handed it to Emma.

"Thank you," Emma said as she placed the bonnet on her head, tidying her hair and wiping the sweat from her face. Before she could do much more, she heard the bark of Mrs. Jones as the portly woman entered the room.

"Jonathan, your waistcoat is a shambles. This is not some back alley, go get it changed now," Mrs. Jones hollered.

Emma felt her feet freeze to the floor and her tongue felt thick and unruly in her throat. As she had raced across London, she had imagined herself having this conversation. In her head, it had seemed so easy. But as the red-faced and angry housekeeper approached her, she could no longer form a coherent thought.

"Whatever happened to you, girl?" Mrs. Jones barked as she stood with her hands on her hips and shook her head. "I will not have you coming here looking like this. My goodness, if the mistress was to see you, I am sure she would send me packing for allowing such a ruffian in her house."

Emma knew that her mouth was opening and closing, the words just would not come. Mary patted her on the shoulder and that seemed to work.

"I'm so sorry, Mrs. Jones. My mama is dreadfully sick. I ran here as quickly as I could to ask that she be allowed the day off, and may I go purchase some medicine for her."

"This will not be," Mrs. Jones said.

It was her favourite phrase when something happened that she did not like. It was almost as if she thought that denying something could prevent it from happening.

"You are telling me that I will be down two maids today. How am I supposed to cope?"

Emma shook her head for she did not know.

"Answer me, girl, give me one reason why I should let either of you return when you have let me down so badly?"

Emma felt the world falling out from under her. They still struggled for money. When her mother got better, if she had lost her job, how would they pay the rent? How would they pay for food? No, she had to do something about this. It was her responsibility to keep her mother safe and of course David. "If you will allow me, I will take my mother the medicine and I will come back. I will work as long as you need me. I will work every day until my mother is well again."

Mrs. Jones huffed and shook her head. Emma was sure she was going to deny her this request. That she was going to make her work a full day. By the time she left, the apothecary would be closed, and her mother would have been without medicine for all those hours. What should she do? Should she leave the job and try to get another? So many questions were buzzing around her brain like a swarm of angry and confused flies, and Mrs. Jones was just staring at her. Emma felt tears form at the back of her eyes. The last thing she wanted, was for Mrs. Jones to see her crying.

"Oh, for goodness sake, child," Mrs. Jones said, but her voice was not as harsh as normal. "Take your mother the medicine, make sure she gets it, and then come back here ready for us to prepare the midday meal. You will work to your normal time today. And you will work the full week while your mother is off, as long as she doesn't need you. Now run along, I will not have a weeping child in my kitchen."

Emma curtsied and swallowed down the lump in her throat. "Thank you, thank you so much, Mrs. Jones. You are an angel, thank you…."

"Get along now, girl, before I change my mind," Mrs. Jones said and Emma could have sworn there was a grin on her face.

Emma gave Mary a quick smile before she turned and fled from the kitchen. As she raced back down the streets that she had only just run. and a horrible empty feeling filled her insides. Would she be in time? Would the medicine help?

As she sped along the streets, tears streamed from her eyes, but she did not slow down for fear that she would be too late.

CHAPTER 5

Soon, Emma found herself inside the apothecary's store. It was filled with strange jars teeming with things she had never seen. The man behind the counter was an austere looking chap with long grey sideburns and a moustache that seemed to join to them. As she looked around, he was pouring liquid from a black bottle into a glass jar. With his pristine white shirt, red waistcoat and bowtie, gold pocket watch, and a black bowler, he looked all too unapproachable to her.

On the counter was a jar of leaches, a brass weighing scale, with the weights lined up in front of it. Once more she froze and clutched onto her apron, for she did not know what to say, what to ask for. And all this time that she was wasting, her dear mama could be getting worse.

"Can I help you, miss?" the apothecary said in a very friendly voice.

Emma nodded and her tears began to fall.

"Oh, oh, dearie, dearie me," the apothecary said as he stepped out from behind the counter. Soon he was in front of Emma and offering her a pristine white handkerchief. Emma clasped onto it and dabbed at her eyes.

"Now, my dear, what can I do for you?"

He gave her a smile that was friendly and open and made her feel suddenly welcome. For just a moment she wondered if her father would look as kind as this man. Pushing that thought aside she tried to gain her thoughts.

"My dear mama has a terrible cough," she said.

"I'm sure we can help her. Describe her symptoms to me as best as you can." Once more he gave her a smile and then he turned to walk back behind his counter.

Emma offered him the handkerchief back.

"Please, keep it."

Emma nodded and swallowed once more as she took another dab at her eyes. "She has a terrible cough. Sometimes she coughs up a little blood. She is soaked in sweat and not too steady on her feet. Well, last night she fell and she hasn't been up since. I know she's breathing but I haven't been able to get her to eat or drink."

"You say she is hot and feverish?" he asked.

Emma nodded.

"Perhaps her skin is a little red?"

Emma tried her hardest to think. Was her mama's skin red? Maybe it was, just a touch. It was hard to tell in the dingy rooms they lived in, with just a few candles to light their way. But now the more that she thought about it, the more she thought that it was. So she nodded again.

"Then I have a diagnosis for you. Your mama has scarlet fever."

Before Emma could take this in, the man before her was already rummaging through the jars on his shelves and humming a little to himself. This was quite disconcerting for she had heard of the scarlet fever and it was vicious, and killed many who contracted it. Still, the apothecary did not seem worried. He selected one large jar filled with a white liquid, and then another much smaller empty jar. Soon he was pouring the white milky liquid from the larger to the smaller. He sealed the top and slapped it down on the counter. Then he got another wide-bottomed jar and filled it with a liquid. Taking a pair of pincers out from under the counter, he fished out six leaches and sealed them into the jar.

"Now, you are to give your mother two drops of this." He picked up the smaller jar. "It is laudanum and it will help with any pain, the fever, and it will help her to sleep. You can give it every six hours, just place the drops on her tongue."

He stopped and looked at her. Emma nodded to let him know she understood.

"You must apply these," he picked up the bottle of leaches and shook them. "Three to her left thigh and three to her left arm. Let them drink for thirty minutes. If they are lazy, rub the area with a little milk or wine. They will draw the poison away from her heart and allow her to heal. If after the thirty minutes they do not drop off, apply a little salt and they will surely do so. After each treatment, place them back in the solution. You may use them for three days, if after that time there is no improvement come and see me again."

"Thank you." Emma reached out to take the bottles but he put his hand on them to stop her.

"That will be one guinea, my dear," he said with a smile.

Emma gulped, it was a lot of their money, but she had no choice. Pulling her coin purse from her pocket she counted out the pence and shillings to make up the guinea. It was almost all she had, at least this week's rent was paid and she would get her wages at the end of the week. With luck there would be enough to pay the rent with the savings her mama had under the loose floorboard.

Handing over the money, she watched while he counted, once he was happy, he took his hand off the bottles.

"I wish your dear mama well," he said with a big smile. "May God bless 'er soul."

Emma had come out without her basket, so she placed the small bottle in the pocket of her apron and held onto the other one tightly. The journey home would be much more sedate than the one to get here. She could not afford to drop and smash the bottle, for if she did her mother was surely dead.

Back at the house Emma found her mother was unresponsive. Though she was breathing, she did not respond to Emma's calls or shakes. David was worried. Normally, he would play in his own corner but now he was sitting on the floor next to his mother's bed with his train discarded in his lap.

"Is Mama going to leave us?" he asked.

Emma did not know, but she knew she could not let him worry. "I have the medicine now. She will be fine. All we need to do is keep wiping her brow and I will give her the medicine whenever she needs it." She gave him a small smile but there was moisture in his eyes and a wobble to his lips. Still, he nodded.

"Why don't you go play with your train in the yard for a little while? I have to give mother her treatment."

David looked between Emma and their mother, and she thought for a moment that he would refuse. She understood how he felt. He didn't want to leave her and come back and find that she had gone. Only if she was going to put on the leaches, she didn't want him to see.

"Run along now, she will be fine. I will call you when we are done."

David nodded and the mop of blonde curls cascaded down to cover his face. It squeezed her heart to see him in such pain, but there was nothing she could do now. Taking his train he walked sedately out into the hall. Normally, he would have run, bubbling with joy and energy. Hopefully, the medicine would work and he would soon be happy again.

Now that he was gone, she took the bottle of laudanum out of her apron. With a shaking hand she opened the dropper bottle, only her mother's mouth was closed, what should she do? Feeling so stupid and inadequate she reached down and touched her mother's cheek. It was slick with sweat and yet cold. Knowing she had to act, she parted her mother's lips and placed two drops onto her tongue. All she could hope was that this medicine would help and would give her mother strength. Now she had to do the bit she was really dreading. Only, she had to hurry, for the quicker she got this done the quicker she could get back to work, and the more money they would have to pay the rent.

Quickly, she removed enough of her mother's clothes to apply the leaches. As she unclasped the jar, she was suddenly afraid. The ugly black things repulsed her, and strangely reminded her of the landlord, Mr Cuthbert. For long moments she held her fingers over the jar, unable to reach in and take out the slug like creatures.

Below her on the pallet her mother lay quiet and sweating. Only the slight rise of her chest let Emma know that she was still with them.

She had to do this, for her mother.

Reaching into the jar she picked out the first of the leaches. She could have sworn she heard it shriek as the slippery fat beast squirmed in her fingers. The urge to drop it back into the water was strong, but she ignored it. Controlling the shaking of her fingers she placed it on her mother's left thigh.

For a second it just sat there. An obscene black blob on her mother's pure white flesh. Then, it crept slowly across her skin and then seemed to find the right spot. It sank its head into her flesh and Emma had to bite back the bile that filled her throat.

The next two leaches were placed much easier. Emma knew that leeches were a medical wonder. It was just her own stupidity that was making this so hard. Perhaps it was her lack of education? For she was sure that the apothecary would have had no such problem.

Having removed her mother's blouse she placed three more leaches on her arm. Now all she had to do was wait. So she took the pocket watch that her mother kept on the mantelpiece and sat holding her hand as the time ticked away.

As if they were a medical miracle, as the thirty minutes came near to ending, all but one of the leaches came away. Quickly, but with no less qualms, Emma picked them up and put them back in the jar. After touching each one she wanted to shake her hand and wipe away the slime but she was conscious of the time. She wanted to make sure that she did this as precisely as she was told. The last of the leaches, the third one that she had placed on her mother's thigh, did not want to move. For a moment, she couldn't remember what she was told. Should she pull it? Should she leave it? Panic had raised her pulse and she found she was panting. This was silly, she had to be calm. Then she remembered, salt. Quickly, she crossed to the cupboard where they kept their food and reached in to find the salt. Taking a pinch of the precious commodity, she placed it over the leaches head. The fat black slug pulled back immediately.

Letting out a big breath of air, Emma picked up the now bloated creature and dropped it back into the jar. Then she sealed the jar and placed that and the laudanum at the back of the cupboard far out of David's reach.

All she could do now was stare at her mother. Had there been any change? It didn't appear that there had, but maybe she was expecting too much too soon. So she took a damp cloth and wiped her mother's brow and face. "I love you, Mama," she whispered as she gave her a quick kiss on her forehead.

Calling David back in, she explained that their mother was sleeping and that the medicine would help her. "I have to leave now. I have to go back to work. If Mama wakes up there is bread-and-butter that you can give her and you can heat up a little bit of stew. There is plenty there for you too."

This brought a bit of a smile to his face and he nodded and waved his train.

"I will be back as soon as I can, but I might have to work later. You are the man of the house now; you have to look after both of you until I come back. Can you do that?"

David nodded.

Emma pulled him close and kissed the top of his soft curly hair. "I love you, little brother."

CHAPTER 6

Emma ran back to the big house. By the time she got there she was feeling exhausted. Both emotionally and physically and she still had a full day's work ahead of her. She came into the kitchen and was surprised to see Mrs. Jones sitting in the corner, having a cup of tea and a slice of bread and butter.

"I was wondering if you were coming back," Mrs. Jones said, but her voice was not as harsh as normal.

"I'm sorry, Mrs. Jones, I came as quickly as I could."

"How is your mother?"

Emma swallowed down the lump in her throat and fought the tears that wanted to escape her eyes. "I secured her some medicine. She is feverish, but she is resting. I am hopeful that she will recover soon."

"I see." Mrs. Jones nodded. "You look a little hot and dishevelled. It will not do for you to be working in the house looking like that."

Emma's heart sank, was she to be fired anyway?

"Sit with me for a few minutes. You can have a cup of tea and two slices of bread and butter. After that you will wipe your face and tidy your hair before you start your work. I will not expect you to stay extra hours today, but I will expect you to work six days this week. Because you are younger than your mother, I am hoping that you can make up for the fact that we are a maid down."

Emma felt a surge of joy go through her. The housekeeper had never been this nice to anyone and yet here she was helping. This time there was no fighting back the tears of joy. Maybe they had a chance and she could work while her mother regained her strength.

Emma worked hard for six whole days. The week rushed by, despite the constant worry about leaving David and their mother alone. Each night she went home and cooked and looked after David. At the same time she bathed and cleaned their mama and gave her the medicine. Some nights their mama woke for a short while. She was weak and feverish but Emma managed to get a little chicken broth down her. The broth had come from a chicken carcass left from the big house. Cook had let her take it home. With a few vegetables it made a hearty meal and seemed to help.

As the week drew to a close Pamela had woken once more. Only, this time she was delirious. Mumbling apologies, shouting and lashing out. It was heart breaking to watch. Emma didn't know what to do and it scared David so much that he cried the whole night.

"Mama has the devil in her," he sobbed as Emma held him to her shoulder and rubbed his back.

"No, my sweet child, she's just ill, it is just the fever." Emma said the words, but she no longer knew what she believed. When she had gone back to the apothecary, he had just told her to give it more time. Only, her mother was wasting away before her eyes and she knew that soon there would be nothing left of her.

There was another problem, tomorrow she had to pay the rent. Mrs. Jones had paid her a little more each day and she had worked six days. But it was not as much as they were getting for two of them. Would it be enough? How much did they have to pay? Why had she never taken notice of these things? Why had she always hidden away from their landlord?

That night, after David had gone to sleep, she applied the leaches and gave her mother the milky medicine. It seemed to ease her pain and she slept much easier after it. That was something, it had to be.

Before she went to bed, she pulled up the loose floorboard and counted the money. By the time she had done all the shopping, she hoped there would be just enough left. They needed candles, and kerosene, and coal just to cook and to see at night. They were also getting low on food and tea. Of course, their mother would often stop at the market as she walked back from work. That way she would pick up items each day. Emma had been rushing back and forth so quickly that she hadn't thought of it. The cupboard was running low and she had to shop soon.

Suddenly, she realized how much her mother had had to cope with and she felt selfish for not helping out earlier. How could she have been so happy when their mama had so much on her mind? Placing the coins into the hidey-hole, she put the floorboard back over it, and sat at her mother's bedside. Emma had taken to sleeping on the floor next to her mother. She would hold her hand and curl up and pray that by morning her mother would be well again.

Of course, the next morning nothing had changed. Emma knew this could not go on much longer. That their sweet mama, would simply fade away if something didn't happen soon. Already her bones showed through her paper-thin skin. What could she do?

After a fitful night of little sleep, Emma woke tired and more worried than she could say. Beside her, her mother was quiet but she could see her chest rise and fall. She had made it through another night. Across the room, she could hear David snoring. The sound was music to her ears. It meant that he was sleeping. That he had escaped the worry, at least for a little while.

Emma threw back her blanket and went about her morning chores. It was hard to keep the tears from her eyes but she managed. While she made breakfast, David got up and came and tugged at her skirts. She turned to see tears in his eyes and he hugged on to her. Holding him tight she let her own tears fall.

"It's all right, it's all right," she mumbled into his hair as they sobbed together. Only it wasn't. It never would be again for she knew that their mama was not long for this world.

Like only the very young, David cried out his tears and then he was fine. The pain had been released. Emma sent him out to get washed and fetch in some water. It would keep him busy. As he left, she dropped to her knees and sobbed some more. "Oh papa! Why did you leave us? Why did you abandon us to this?"

"Emma," the voice was frail and from behind her.

"Mama?"

Emma ran to her mother and could see she was trying to sit up. "Mama, are you well? Are you better?" Emma felt a flood of joy. All her hard work had paid off. Her mama was awake and lucid for the first time since the illness. She wanted to shout for David. He always took so long when he went to the toilet and washed in the morning. She didn't want him to miss this.

"I am not better..." The words were interrupted by a weak and moist cough. It sounded like the cough was escaping from a watery grave.

"I will get you some gruel, don't talk, rest." Emma tried to stand but her mother's hand held her back.

"Sweet child... I have to... tell you something," the words were breathy and painful for her to speak.

"No, rest."

Pamela looked up at her daughter. Her eyes were weak and full of tears. "I am so proud of you my sweet girl. You have done everything you could. I don't have long."

"No, Mama, please don't say that."

Pamela shook her head, but the movement was too much for her, and another cough brought with it a touch of blood. "I have to tell you about Benedict... about your papa."

Emma felt both fear and joy. Was she to find out how to contact their father? This could be the answer to all their problems. He would be able to bring the doctor. He would take care of them. Only, her mother was struggling to speak. Her mouth moved and there was a lump in her throat.

"He didn't abandon us," Pamela managed.

Emma took her hand and tried to pass her strength through the contact. Her mama was speaking but the words were too faint to hear. Emma leaned over and listened.

"He had no choice...he..."

The hand dropped from hers and her mama was still. Deathly still. Somehow, Emma knew that it was different this time. That her mother was not resting, not recovering, she was gone. Holding her hand as it began to chill, she let her tears fall.

Their mother was now in Heaven, but they were stuck to deal with their very cruel place on Earth.

CHAPTER 7

Everything felt surreal, like a horrible story told to frighten children and keep them in their place. Emma and David had lain awake all night, both of them on David's tiny mattress, huddled together with their emotions swaying from grief to fear and back again.

Emma knew David was more afraid than anything else. At only nine, his mind was apt to wander in the direction of the idea that there was a cold, dead body in the room with them, sharing the darkness. In truth, Emma had moments in which she felt the same, but her own heartbreak and fears for the future consumed her more.

Emma could feel David shivering in her arms and knew it was more than just fear; he was cold, as was she. Unable to bear the already very obvious odour of her mother's gradual disintegration, Emma had slid open the sash windows and was determined to leave them open until the man came with the cart to take the body of Pamela Mason away. It was early April and by no means warm, but she didn't want the faintly sweet, faintly sour smell to be her last memory of the mother she loved more than life.

She'd done everything in her power to avoid it, working through her own tears to wash down her mother's body and dress her in an old and worn but clean dress. She had tied a thick swathe of cotton fabric around her mother's chin and head, ensuring that her mouth did not gape open and terrify David.

The clothes she had died in were already thrown away for Emma could never bear to look at them again. She knew her mother would have been annoyed with her for sending good material to the grave, but Emma was determined her mother meet her maker in the best she had. As for her other few stitches of clothing, Emma would make alterations to them and wear them eventually. Waste not, want not, that was something Pamela Mason had said often.

"Emma, I'm so cold," David mumbled, his voice sounding tiny and tired.

"I know, I'm sorry," she replied, taking her shawl from around her shoulders and wrapping it around her little brother. She immediately felt the chill deep in her bones, but it was her idea to have the place fresh and she would live with the consequences. David was her responsibility now. Everything was her responsibility. Tears sprang to her already sore and aching eyes. How could her mother be gone? How was it that they were alone in the world? A girl of not yet sixteen and a little boy of nine. With no grandparents nor even aunts or uncles, they were truly orphans now. But they were not alone in that, were they? Half the ragamuffins who walked the streets of London were either true orphans, runaways, or those who had been discarded by drunken and dreadful parents to fend for themselves in the world.

Holding David, who was now sleeping, tighter to her, Emma made a silent vow that she would never let David wander the streets the way so many other young orphans did. She would work twice as hard now, twice as long if Martha Jones would let her, and they would manage somehow. She would pay the rent and they would continue to strive and struggle until something happened to change all of that. Of course, she knew that by *something happening*, she really meant that fine young hero of her girlish daydreams. The man who would marry her and take her away from the misery and the poverty, rescuing her angelic little brother into the bargain.

However, as she lay in the darkness, shivering and with tears rolling down her cheeks, rescue seemed like a very long way away.

∾

It was almost midday when the man arrived with the cart. Emma had risen early, having only slept for an hour or so, and had raced to the big house to tell Martha Jones what had happened. Once again, Martha was cautiously kind, looking over her shoulder to be sure they were alone before taking Emma into her arms and giving her a brief but firm embrace. She had told Emma to take the next day to herself too, but Emma had bravely proclaimed she would return to work the following day. How could she not? The rent would be due in just a day or two and she still didn't know how much it was or if she had enough coin to cover it. And everything would be done by the end of the day, wouldn't it? Her mother would be gone; unceremoniously tipped into a pauper's grave without so much as a wooden cross to show that Pamela Mason had ever walked this earth.

"All right, little miss," the man with the cart had only tapped lightly on the door before opening it and popping his head around the edge. "I've come for the…" he paused, and she knew he had been about to say *the body*. "Your mother." He looked kind and sorry for her.

"Thank you," Emma said, giving him an exhausted smile. "You will be careful with her, won't you?"

"Of course, I will, love. I've been doing this a long time, too long, to be honest, so you have no fears at all. I'll make sure your mother's last journey is a decent one, I promise."

"And I should pay you now, shouldn't I?"

"If you would. It's a shilling," he said and looked regretful, although Emma knew his life was probably no easier than her own and he undoubtedly needed the money.

Emma had the money in a little cloth purse in the pocket of her dress and she fished it out to pay him.

"How will you manage to get down the stairs?" Emma asked, having a sudden and awful image of having to help the man carry her mother's lifeless body down to the cart.

"Not to worry, love, the landlord has already said he will lend me a hand. I normally have my boy with me, but his mother's sick and I had to leave him with her."

"I'm so sorry. I hope your wife will soon recover."

"Well, it's scarlet fever," he said and looked down.

"Then please take this," Emma said, opening the cupboard where the leeches still bobbed in their glass jar and the laudanum, still half-full, remained. "There's no sense in just throwing it all away." She handed the jars to him and he looked grateful.

"Thank you," he said, seeming taken aback by her kindness on such an awful day. "I'll just put these in the cart so as not to break them on the way."

Emma nodded as the man hurried out and down the stairs. She turned to David, who was looking at the body of their mother lying on the bed.

"I don't want to never see her again," he said and began to cry.

"I know, David. But Mama has to go now. It's time for her to be with the angels again." Emma took him into her arms, his little blond head resting against her as he sobbed. "We have to be brave for Mama now." She leaned forward and kissed the top of his head.

Hearing footsteps, slow and laborious, Emma knew that it wasn't the returning cart man but Jairus Cuthbert. She shuddered before a thought occurred to her. She raced across the room, leaving David a little stunned and open-mouthed, then pulled up the floorboard and hurriedly retrieved all the money they had before setting the board to rights. She would pay the rent a day early and in the presence of the cartman.

"Well, it looks like I'm going to have to help get her down the stairs," was the first thing Jairus said upon entering the room. "Not that she ever gave me an ounce of respect whilst she was alive."

"Thank you, Mr Cuthbert," Emma said, holding back the worst of her anger; what a hateful thing to say. But she knew that she needed to keep on the right side of this awful man and railing against his spite would do nothing to help her and David now.

He lumbered further into the room, his slicked-back hair and beady eyes reminding her once again of the rat she had watched with such interest all those weeks before; a time when she'd had no idea of the heartbreak to come. He paused, looking her up and down without any hint of respect for the day, for her loss. It made her shiver.

"So, all alone in the world now, eh?" He actually smiled and Emma felt bile rising in her throat.

At that moment, the healthier, faster footsteps of the cartman could be heard, and Emma let go of her anxious breath. She was safe for now, at least.

"Mr Cuthbert, thank you," the cartman said as he walked into the room. "As I said, I normally have my boy with me."

"Very well. Very well," Jairus said in a tone of annoyance and Emma knew that he was angry to be interrupted rather than angry at the prospect of a few minutes' work.

"Oh, since you're here, Mr Cuthbert," Emma said, taking her money from her pocket and making ready to put her plan of self-preservation into action. "I'm afraid I don't know what my mama paid for rent, but if you would be kind enough to tell me, I shall pay it now." She realised the plan was two-fold; she would be spared time alone with Jairus and his awful glances, and she would know if he hiked up the rent price, for surely the cartman as a witness would know what was a sensible rent and what was not.

"Five shillings and sixpence," he barked, and looked daggers at her; he knew she was playing a game; she could see it in those rat-like beady eyes.

She cast a surreptitious glance at the cartman who clearly saw nothing extraordinary in the stated price, and so she hurriedly counted out the coins exactly and handed them to Jairus. She avoided his direct gaze, knowing that the anger she could feel rolling off him in waves would be horribly plain to see there.

"Right, let's get on with this," Jairus said, tipping his head in the direction of Pamela Mason's lifeless body.

At that moment, David began to sob and Emma, for the time being at least, forgot all about Jairus Cuthbert.

Emma and David stood side by side as their mother, now in a flimsily constructed coffin, was lowered into the ground. The grave was deep and already contained several other such coffins; the bodies of the poor who could not afford seventeen shillings for anything better being laid to rest together. The grave diggers bid the two forlorn children to move back, for they were about to throw down some powdered lime and it wouldn't do to get it in their eyes.

Emma knew what the lime was for but was glad David didn't. It was to halt the spread of infectious diseases, for the grave would not yet be covered with earth until more dead were thrown in, their own flimsy coffins almost reaching the surface. David, shattered and pale, didn't need to know that his mother would be laying there so exposed for days until more people died.

A clergyman from the church hurried out and gave no more than a few hurried sentences to see Pamela Mason into the world beyond. Emma knew folks with money had better from their men of God, but at least this was almost a funeral. Her mother hadn't been discarded entirely.

When Emma finally walked away, clutching tightly to David's hand, she realised that the cartman had waited. He was just replacing his battered flat cap, a sure sign that he had given a moment of silent reflection for the passing of a woman he had never known. Emma wondered if he did so for all the poor souls he transported to their final destination, or if he had made her mother a special case. Either way, it was a small comfort to her. It was a gentle reminder that there were still good men in the world.

The cartman nodded sadly before taking his leave and Emma smiled at him before continuing to make her way home. Home; would it ever feel like home again? She doubted it. If only they were not alone. Surely, they could not be orphans whilst their father still lived. But was he still alive? If only her mother had been able to finish those final words. *He had no choice...*

Where was he? How could he not know his beloved wife was dead and his children alone and in great need of him? If only she knew more. Even to know he was truly dead would at least stop her wondering if he was ever coming back.

CHAPTER 8

"Don't stay out here all day. And don't wander off with any other lads; they'll lead you into trouble, do you hear me?" Emma knew her tone was a little hard, but she knew she must carry on where her mother left off as far as David was concerned.

He would soon be ten and Emma knew well that boys of that age could so easily be led astray. She could hardly think of the trouble he could get into whilst she was away all day working for Mr and Mrs Hastings in the big house on Russell Square. More than once, she had imagined returning home and being unable to find him, later discovering that he had been arrested for some crime of stupidity that would ruin his life or even see him sent away. No, she had to be firm but be kind, she had to be his mother now.

"I don't want to be in the house all day, Emma. It still feels funny and I don't like it," his bottom lip jutted out and began to wobble and she knew, without a doubt, that the memory of their mother's lifeless body lying on the bed through a day and a night had still not left him.

Of course, it had only been two days since the awful sight of her mother being lowered into a pauper's grave. Surely, it would take longer than that for either one of them to forget the bone jarring horror of it all.

"Leave the poor lad alone, you ain't his mother," the rough voice was accompanied by a humorous laugh and Emma spun around to see the costermonger, a man commonly known as Spuddy, grinning at her, the one tooth he was so very proud of on full display.

"No, I'm not his mother. His mother is not here anymore, Spuddy," Emma bit back waspishly.

"I know that, don't I?! I wasn't meaning nothing by it, was I?! Reckon the poor kid is sad enough without you making him sit alone inside four walls all day long, that's all," Spuddy said and shrugged somewhat disarmingly.

"I don't want him getting into any trouble. He doesn't have anybody to look out for him now but me and I'll thank you to keep your nose to yourself." Emma was riding high on her dignity, something which seemed to amuse Spuddy greatly.

"All right, Duchess, keep your hair on!" he said and gave a long, low whistle, something which that single tooth seemed somehow unlikely to allow for. "And I was sorry to hear about your mother, I really was. She used to buy a few bits from me now and again and she was always nice. A sight warmer than you are, anyway," he went on, smiling at her, teasing her.

"Thank you," Emma said and felt her shoulders drop. She hadn't meant to bite his head off, she was just so anxious about the future, about David's future.

"Look, the boy can come and work for me if he likes," Spuddy said, surprising her with the change in conversational direction. "Got a good voice, has he? A man gets tired of bellowing about his own wares all day long. What do you reckon, little scrap? Got a pair of lungs, have you?" He turned to look at David who had inched further towards them both.

"I have, do you want me to shout now? I can show you how loud I can be," David said, his eyes lighting up and his face seeming to be that of a child for the first time in days.

"Oh, I don't know…" Emma said, feeling suddenly on the spot and completely taken aback. "He's not even ten years old," she went on.

"By which time most young lads already have three years' work under their little belts, Duchess." He shook his head slowly from side to side but was still smiling at her, seeming to enjoy the nickname he'd given her. "And I dare bet you could use the coin, couldn't you? It won't be much, mind, but not much is better than nothing, ain't it?"

"Please, Emma," David said, already leaning his hands on the top of the wooden cart, his eyes roaming over the apples, potatoes, and turnips in crates on the top. "I don't want to be by myself all day," he added, lowering his voice as if his pride had taken over and he didn't want to appear to be any less of a man in front of Spuddy; Emma could see he already admired the costermonger.

"All right, all right, David," she said, laying a hand on top of his springy blonde curls. "But you see that you do everything that Spuddy tells you, all right? You make sure you behave yourself, promise me," she went on, looking into his large, angelic blue eyes.

"I promise," he said in a whisper, his pale cheeks turning a little pink; his sister was embarrassing him.

"Like I said, it won't be much, but it will keep him out of trouble, won't it?" Spuddy went on, keen to confirm that his kindness wasn't going to cost him an arm and a leg.

"Thank you, Spuddy. And I'm sorry if I was a bit harsh with you. These last few days have been, well, I daresay you already know."

"I suppose we all know what it is to lose somebody, Duchess. The hard part is knowing how to keep going. What else can we do?" He smiled again, that solitary tooth seeming almost like a friend now.

"I'd better get going," she said, smiling back at Spuddy before leaning forward to kiss the top of David's head. "And remember what I said, David. And if you're finished before I get back, then please go inside the house."

"Don't you worry, we'll still be here when you get back from the big house," Spuddy said and grinned at David. "Right, let's get to your learning," he added and boomed with laughter.

As she walked away, Emma felt the first measure of relief she'd felt for days. She was certain that Spuddy was far from a respectable man, but he seemed to be kind enough and he was the first person who had offered any sort of real help. He'd had his cart there at the little market for as long as she could remember, so Emma thought that she could be sure he would really keep David out of trouble. And when she heard David's childlike voice booming in the distance, the words *"Wi-ild rabbits, two a shilling,"* followed by *"Penny a bunch of turnips,"* she couldn't help but smile to herself; maybe things really would be all right in the end.

"I'm sorry I'm late, Mrs Jones," Emma said as she hurried into the scullery, quickly discarding her shawl and replacing it with the thick cotton apron.

"You're not late, child, but I'll accept your apology if you're so determined to make it," Martha Jones seemed faintly amused.

"Oh dear, I assumed I was late. I got talking to the costermonger in Clerkenwell and I haven't got my mother's pocket watch with me," Emma went on, breathlessly explaining.

"You have another full day ahead of you, Emma. The maids have taken all the sheets off the beds today, so getting them all washed and out on the line will keep you busy."

"Good, I'm glad," Emma said and meant it. She wanted a day of busyness, a day of plunging her roughened hands into the water as she scrubbed the sheets clean. It would be her second day back at work and she'd never been more grateful for the prospect of the backbreaking grind. It wasn't just the money she was earning; it was leaving behind her sadness and fear for a while.

"Are you quite all right, my dear?" Martha Jones asked, looking over her shoulder first as she always did. No doubt she didn't want the other young women, the maids and the scullery maids, knowing that she had a softer side.

"Yes, thank you, Mrs Jones. I just think that washing sheets will help me to forget everything for a little while."

"You've had a rotten time of it right enough, but I can't say I'm not glad to see you back again. It might be a while before we get somebody to replace your mother and we're already falling behind here." Martha said and Emma realised that she didn't despise her in the way that she had despised Jairus Cuthbert.

Martha Jones wasn't being cruel or intentionally disrespectful, this was just how life was for people of their class. Everything had to keep moving, the wealthy could never be expected to do for themselves, after all.

"I don't mind working longer hours and extra days, Mrs Jones. To be honest, without Mama's wage, I really need the money." Emma decided to simply be honest; what good would it do to let pride take over now?

"Well, you can carry on doing the six days a week just as you were doing when your mother first fell ill. Obviously, you won't be paid as much as she was, not at your age, but let's hope it's enough to keep the wolf from the door, shall we?" She gave her another warm smile.

"Thank you, Mrs Jones. Thank you so much," Emma said, fighting back the tears and an urge to throw her arms around the standoffish old housekeeper. "And David will be earning a few coins too, so maybe we really will manage after all," she went on, clearing her throat and determined to maintain her dignity.

"And what will he be doing?" Martha asked cautiously, her face clearly telling Emma that she assumed it to be something shady or even downright illegal; there really weren't so many options for orphans.

"He's going to be working with the costermonger at Clerkenwell. He only started today and I'm just glad that there's somebody to keep an eye on him, to keep him out of trouble. I was so worried leaving a boy of that age on his own all day that he might fall in with the sort of crowd my mama always feared. Pickpockets and what have you," she added, as if Martha Jones really needed it explained to her.

"Well, if it's the costermonger at Clerkenwell, I expect you're talking about Spuddy," Martha said and narrowed her gaze disapprovingly.

"You know him?" Emma asked, suddenly afraid that she had done the wrong thing in entrusting the man with the care of her brother.

"I buy a little of this and that in Clerkenwell now and again, when I'm over that way."

"And what do you think of Spuddy?"

"Don't look so worried, he's no different from so many others of his kind. All cheek and lip, flashing that one tooth of his as if anybody wants to see a smile like that! But I daresay deep down there's a decency to him. Deep down. Which is not to say I would trust him entirely. Whenever I put out my hand to take my change from him, I always count my fingers in case one is missing," Martha said and gave a deep and rumbling laugh; Emma had never heard her laugh before.

There was something infectious about it and Emma found herself laughing too. Largely, she was relieved to discover that Spuddy, despite probably having an edge to him somewhere, was overall trustworthy enough to keep David out of trouble. She knew there would be very little money in it, for had he not already said as much himself. But as he had said, a little was better than nothing and at least she could now relax, relatively safe in the knowledge that David would have someone watching out for him.

"Thank you, Mrs Jones," Emma said, dabbing at the corners of her eyes and knowing that the faint wetness was a mixture of amusement, emotion, and days and days of sadness. "You've put my mind at rest."

"Good, then let's get your rested mind to put your hands to good work, shall we? Chop-chop, you've got a busy day, remember?" Despite her return to sternness, Emma could see the vaguest glint of kindness still hovering in Martha Jones' eyes.

CHAPTER 9

As the end of the week drew near, Emma's mind began to turn to thoughts of paying the rent. There was a part of her that felt a little proud, knowing that she had earned enough and kept enough by her to have the five shillings and sixpence already set aside for that most necessary expense. Not only that, but there would be a little left to buy a few vegetables and some bread.

Martha Jones had begun to make a habit of carefully wrapping meat bones for Emma to take home with her and boil up to make soups and stews with. It certainly was a help, for she had not purchased a single piece of meat for her and her brother to eat since their mother had passed away. Perhaps she would save a coin or two over the next weeks and even buy one of those wild rabbits that Spuddy had her brother bellowing about.

But her pride aside, when Emma thought of paying the rent, fear and revulsion crept into her veins and flew around her body with every heartbeat.

So, when Friday finally came, Emma left David watching the stew hanging on the hook over the fire and made him promise not to let it boil over or burn. She walked slowly down the stairs to where Jairus lived on the ground floor, idly amusing herself that it would have done his health some good to have lived higher up, to exercise that ugly fat body on the stairs.

Emma tapped lightly at the door, almost wishing that he wouldn't answer. But she needed to pay him and to have the ordeal done for another week. She knocked again, louder this time, and tried to imagine the relief she would feel walking away from his door in just a few moments from now.

She could hear Jairus' heavy footsteps crossing the room and braced herself. He was grumbling, muttering under his breath, but she couldn't make out what he was saying. The mumbling stopped when he opened the door and peered out at her. His frown was replaced by a look of sudden self-satisfaction; a look which made her visibly shudder.

"Don't look at me like that, girl! I'm not the Devil!" he boomed but smiled.

He stood back to allow her entrance, but Emma stayed where she was. She held out her hand and opened it to show him the coins.

"I have the rent money, Mr Cuthbert," she said timidly.

"Well, you'll have to come in so I can count it in the light. I can't stand here squinting in the gloom," he said and stared at her.

Emma froze, every fibre of her being telling her to stand her ground or, better still, to run. But no sooner had the thought crossed her mind than Jairus had reached out and seized her arm. She was so surprised that she almost dropped the coins as he propelled her into the grubby room and kicked the door shut behind her.

"Here, take the money," she said, her voice trembling as much as her hands.

"You look at me as if I'm nothing, just like that mother of yours used to. Now, just who do you think you are, eh? Too good for this place, or at least you think so," he said and was clearly getting angry. His beady eyes bore into her and flecks of saliva flew from fat lips as he spoke, making her wince. "And still you go on. Just who do you think you're looking down on, girl?"

"I'm not looking down on anybody, Mr Cuthbert," she said, her heart pounding as she turned and looked towards the door. She would never make it, she knew that, and he still held her arm tightly in his large, damp hand. "I have just come to pay the rent that is all."

"Come to just pay the rent is it?" Mr Cuthbert's voice held a spite in it that Emma was terrified by. He didn't seem to simply be berating her, but every single person that had every wronged him, every single person that had ever – supposedly – looked down on him. "I always asked your mother this, but since she's cold in the ground, I guess I can ask you straight now. Miss Emma, will you be my wife?"

Emma was taken aback by the question. It seemed so at odds with this man's hateful tone. She could see tears forming in the corners of his eyes.

"You don't have to say anything, I already know your answer." Mr Cuthbert raged on. "I know I disgust you! I disgusted my last wife too, but that never stopped her from showing some respect, even if it was just a crumb of it. That's more than you or your mother ever showed me though!"

Mr Cuthbert lunged forward, and before Emma could do anything, one of his sprawling hands was clasped tightly around her throat. She tried to let out a scream, but no air could escape.

He pulled her in closer to him, and she could feel his warm putrid breath on her face. "You think you're so much better than me, don't you! You don't believe I deserve someone in my life, to love! Maybe I should just take what's owed to me, just like I take your rent money!"

"No!" Emma rasped through the chokehold. "I don't think any of that! I just- I just wanted to pay the rent and leave. I'm..." Emma could feel her vision going fuzzy, as her brain reacted to the lack of air. Her lungs burned. "I'm only fifteen, Mr... I can't marry..."

"Can't, or won't!" Mr Cuthbert demanded. He dragged her across the room in his fury. "Don't lie to me! You hate me, don't you?"

"You're crazy!" Emma managed to scrape out. It was by no means the smartest thing to say, but she couldn't think of anything else. It was getting hard to think.

Mr Cuthbert's wrath boiled over at her accusation. He screeched almost like an animal, and threw her across the room. She slammed into the wall, her face and left hip crunching against it, and she crumpled to the floor.

She tried rising, but a striking pain coursed down her left leg, and her left eye was already matted with blood that was gushing from a wound on her head; she could already feel her face swelling from the impact too. She fell again from her weak attempt to rise.

Mr Cuthbert screamed again enraged. "Look at what you made me do now, you pitiful seductress! You harlot!" He grabbed her by her hair. Her throat felt so red raw she couldn't even cry out. Mr Cuthbert dragged her back towards his door. He slammed it open, and threw her out. "Stay away from me! You little worm!"

He slammed the door behind him. Emma was thankful that it at least meant her assault was over. She took in a breath, and winced at another stabbing pain in her chest. She had small cuts all over, as well as a serious gouge on her head.

Emma crawled her way back to their impoverished little room, only just managing to pull herself up on the door handle to open it, and fell inside with a dull thud. David, playing on the floor with his train, looked up at her, startled by her sudden and noisy entrance.

"Emma?" David said, looking at her with his big blue eyes.

"It's all right, David. It will all be all right soon," she said, her voice sounding like glass scrapping across metal. "Just help me… I need to…" Her brain was fuzzy again, and her vision seemed to fade in and out.

"You're hurt! Real bad!" David cried out, jumping up and discarding his train.

"I know." Emma did her best to stay conscious. "I'm going to need your help to clean and dress my wounds. Can you help me?"

David nodded, and waited for his first order.

Emma didn't know how, but the two siblings were able to stop the bleeding on her forehead and clean her wounds with hot water. It wasn't perfect, but it was the best they could manage.

David helped Emma to her bed, tears still streaming down his face. "Who did this to you?"

"It doesn't…" Emma could already feel sleep invading her body now that she was on her bed. "Please just… lock the door…" And with that, Emma let the blackness take her, an escape from the searing pain in her head and hip.

As she drifted away, the last thing she heard was David praying as he sobbed. "Don't let her go too! Please God, don't let her go too!"

CHAPTER 10

Three weeks later, Emma was walking slowly back home from the big house. Her face had begun to return to normal, Martha Jones had very kindly aided Emma in covering the bruise each day. There was nothing that could be done about her hip though. At first, putting any weight on her left leg had been agony. Now there was still some sharp stabs of pain sporadically, but she could at least walk, albeit with a limp. Mrs Jones had gravely commented that she didn't know if the limp would ever go away. Mr Cuthburt had left his permanent mark on Emma.

When she reached the market, she began to tense. Every step which brought her closer to the place she called home was painful to her, frightening. She dreaded bumping into Jairus Cuthbert anywhere, even in the crowded Clerkenwell Street where she ought to have been reasonably safe from him.

Emma had hardly slept since the attack, waking up every night in a cold sweat from some awful dream or other in which her mind most determinedly relived every awful moment she had suffered. It was Wednesday already, just two days before she was due to pay the rent again. She would have sent David if she did not fear for his safety.

Emma felt as if she were trapped in a nightmare. There was no hope of escape from the nausea inducing fear and remembrance. No wonder her mother had always shown such disdain for that awful man. Emma felt truly abandoned.

As far as she was concerned, any further meetings with that dreadful landlord would have similar outcomes. Should she give in to his demands? Should she marry him? Emma felt as if her capacity to choose was shrinking and shrinking. She closed her eyes and swallowed down the bile; she would rather be dead than marry that man.

She could see the costermonger's cart in the distance and squinted, hoping that there would be a few potatoes and a turnip or two that she could buy from Spuddy and add to the chicken carcass she carried under her arm. It was clear that Martha Jones knew that something terribly wrong had happened to Emma, though she had never asked Emma for any details. A look in the lady's eyes told Emma that perhaps she wasn't the first girl to have gone through such turmoil under Mrs Jones's watch. Whatever she did or did not think, the little gifts of bones and carcasses neatly wrapped were made with ever increasing regularity.

Emma could hardly believe that she had come to see a gentler side to Martha Jones. Her quick temper and easy exasperation was still often in evidence, even with Emma herself. But there was more to Martha than her gruff exterior and austerity of softness. It was a constant source of amazement that there was a real human being resident within the hard exterior. Emma wasn't so naïve to assume Martha to be a friend, but she was no longer an enemy who cared nothing for her. Their relationship was hard to describe in Emma's own head, but she knew she drew some comfort from it.

If only they were close enough for Emma to be able to confide in her, to tell her the very worst of it and hear what she had to say on the matter. She knew Martha to be capable and practical; would she be able to help her, to tell her what to do for the best?

Emma closed her eyes and tried to remember just how much bread they had left in the little tin. Surely, it was almost half a loaf, certainly enough for the meal that evening and something to fill their bellies before they set off again in the morning for a long day's work.

How strange it was that in one moment all she could imagine was the dreadful attack, all she could feel was the fear of what the next few days would bring. In the next moment, her mind was fully occupied with the day-to-day matters of survival, of eating, of working, of simply living. The moments in which her mind was free to think about such mundane things were few and far between, each episode so short lived and greatly missed the moment it left her. But at all times, the limp was ever-present, slowing her down, bearing down on her.

Once again, her mind was filled with the sight of Jairus Cuthbert's evil face just inches away from her. The mental picture was so real that she could almost feel his hand covering her mouth. How she longed to be floating in the air, nothing to touch her, not even a breeze to be felt. How she wanted to feel nothing, to have no physical senses at all. No touch, no smell, no sight. Nothing. She wanted to feel nothing; she wanted to be nothing.

With a deep sigh, Emma began to walk again. She needed to do something about this. She needed to let go of these dreadful imaginings and be a proper guardian to David. He knew that his sister had been hurt, and Emma suspected he knew exactly who had done it too.

In the moment that tears of anger and injustice sprang to her eyes, Emma was distracted by shouts in the distance. There was an excited rumble of chatter filling the gaps between the shouts. She could see people gathering, moving together, a mixture of shock and excitement hanging heavy in the air. Her heart began to thump as she quickened her pace and searched the crowd for any sign of David.

~

Emma spotted Spuddy first, watching him as he formed part of a small group of men talking quickly and loudly. She was almost running by the time she reached him, breathlessly reaching out to touch his arm.

"All right, Duchess?" Spuddy said, his single tooth prominent and his eyes wide and excited. "What's the matter with you?"

"David," she said, trying to get her breath back. "Where's David? What's happening? Is he safe?"

"He's right here, look!" Spuddy said and continued to smile at her. "Didn't I tell you I wouldn't let anything happen to him?"

"Yes, you did. Sorry, Spuddy, but what has happened? Why is everybody shouting? What's all the fuss?" she asked, firing questions at him as if from a cannon.

"The peelers are here, Duchess. They've just gone running into the tavern right enough, throwing people out right, left, and centre to boot," he began, relishing the chance to be the first to tell her the tale. "Someone's been cut to ribbons in there apparently. Dead he is, stone dead," he continued, his eyes getting wider and wider with every word.

"David, David!" she said, taking her eyes off Spuddy for a moment to reach out a hand towards David. The boy looked set to wander in the direction of the tavern and the idea of it made her panic. "Come here!"

With a very obvious sigh, David sauntered over to his sister and reluctantly took her hand. He was a little man now, or so he thought, and he most certainly didn't want to hold his big sister's hand in public.

"I only wanted a look," David said sullenly.

"A look? At a man who has been murdered? David, what has got into you?" Emma could hardly believe what she was hearing, and she looked at her angelic little brother with startled confusion. It momentarily wiped her mind of all her other problems as nothing else could have done.

"It's only Jairus Cuthbert. What do I care if he suffered?" David said with sudden aggression.

"It's... It's...?" Emma stuttered before turning to look at Spuddy for confirmation. "You're absolutely sure? It really is him? And he's dead?"

"That's what they're saying. I don't imagine anybody's made a mistake for who else looks like that ugly old walrus?" Spuddy said and the few men gathered around him began to laugh.

"And the police are in there? They are in the tavern?" Her heart was pounding; Emma hardly dared to hope that this was true. She couldn't stop to think about the right and wrong of all of it. Emma knew that she had wanted the dreadful man dead, that she would have done it by her own hand if she'd had means to do so that awful night. And even now, as she stood there wondering what sort of person this made her, even as she felt how unrighteous her thoughts were, she could feel no remorse, no regret. All she could do was hope with all her heart that the cold dead body of Jairus Cuthbert would soon be brought out of the tavern for all to see.

"They are indeed in there, Duchess. Let go of the boy, for goodness sake, he only wants a little fun." Spuddy laughed again as his male contemporaries wandered away clearly in hopes of having a better view of things.

"No, I don't want him to see this. David, please go into the house, I beg you." She turned to look down at David, still holding his hand and laying her free hand on the soft pale skin of his cheek. "Please."

"I won't go over there, Emma. Just let me stay out, I don't want to miss it."

"Miss what, David, the sight of a man lying dead? No, absolutely not," she said sharply as Spuddy chuckled.

"Then why don't you take him indoors, Duchess? Why don't you go with him?" Spuddy said, eyeing her curiously.

"I need to stay right where I am," she said, knowing that she would not believe that evil fat rat of a man to be dead unless she saw him with her own two eyes.

"Ah, so you don't want to let the boy have his fun, but you intend to do so for yourself!" Spuddy stated, looking pleased with himself as if he had alighted upon some rather clever determination.

"I have my reasons." Her voice was low and without tone of any kind as she held Spuddy's gaze. For his part, Spuddy looked back at her, his eyes opening a little wider as she saw realisation dawning. She knew; he'd realised it right there and then without her having to say a word.

"Right then, you better do as the Duchess says, little man!" Spuddy said, turning to David and reaching for an apple from the cart. "And here, take this with you, it will keep you company. Now, you mind and be a good boy and I'm sure your sister will be back in the house before you know it. Go now, get along," he said, handing David the apple and giving him a gentle shove in the direction of home.

"Thank you," Emma said, feeling a swell of competing emotions swirling in her stomach, not the least of them gratitude. "He does listen to you, Spuddy, he minds what you tell him."

"That's just young lads for you, Duchess. Now then, are you going to get a little bit closer, try to see in through the tavern windows?" he asked, his voice low and his eyebrows raised.

"No, there are peelers all around the outside, look. They're stopping people peering in. I don't suppose they'd let me have a look, would they?" she said and shrugged, realising that she might have a long wait ahead of her. But regardless of how long it was before they brought that body out, Emma knew that she would not move from the spot.

"Ah, but they're only trying to stop them as don't pay for it, ain't they?" Spuddy said with a wicked chuckle. "You know what the peelers are like. Press a coin into their hand and they'll walk you right by him as he lays there in all his gore."

"Will they?" Emma questioned, turning to look at him, her face all innocence and her heart blacker than it had ever been. Even the revelation that a person might pay to be walked through a hideous crime scene didn't permeate the heavy fog of emotional miasma swirling around her.

"He really hurt you, didn't he?" Spuddy said, every ounce of humour now gone and his face more solemn and serious than she had ever known it in all their acquaintance.

Emma couldn't speak, she simply held his gaze and nodded, tears filling her eyes. Spuddy looked down for a moment, a mixture of embarrassment and pity clouding his face as he reached into his pocket. Without a word, he pressed a sixpence into her palm and nodded at her.

Emma looked at him for a moment, slowly realising what he meant for her to do. When he turned and tipped his head in the direction of the tavern, she nodded at him, smiling her thanks as the tears rolled down her face and the words wouldn't come. And then she turned and began to walk towards the policeman ahead of her.

CHAPTER 11

The new landlord of the rundown Clerkenwell tenement building was in place within two days, all ready for the rents to be collected. Myron Appleby was tall and lean with a look of absolute piety on his face which gave Emma some comfort.

She didn't like him at all, but at least he looked at the world around him as if he simply couldn't bear to touch it, and that was just fine by her. There was a wife, too, Vera Appleby was starched upright with even more piety than her husband, but Emma didn't care. There would be no dragging her into the rotten little room on the ground floor when the time came to pay the rent. To be doubly sure, Emma decided to be certain that Mrs Appleby was around whenever she approached to make the payment.

Her first encounter with Mr and Mrs Appleby was less than auspicious, however. There had come a loud knock at the door just minutes after Emma had returned from the big house on Friday in the early evening.

Emma's heart skipped a beat and her stomach had lurched as she immediately imagined that Jairus Cuthbert stood on the other side, his beady eyes glazed over. Even though she had seen his bloated body in all its gore laying twisted against the wall of the tavern, right next to the fireplace, still, her first instinct on hearing that knock was fear.

Swallowing down nausea, Emma cautiously crossed the room to the door. She pictured Jairus as she had last seen him, not to mention the surprised face of the young peeler who had taken her sixpence and led her into the tavern for a quick glance at the horror within. The poor young man had studied her as she peered coldly down at the ugliest man she had ever known, the floorboards around him soaked with his own blood. She had breathed a sigh of relief and smiled. Not a care for what the policeman thought of the girl, not yet a woman, who had the grit to stand and stare at such a sight with a faint smile of relief on her face. But then, if he'd ever been a girl alone in the world, he might have understood it better.

The door was knocked again, this time with even more insistence. Emma quickly opened it to see her new landlord there before her. His angular and unamused wife was by his side with her arm raised as if ready to knock again. So, she was the one who knocked on the doors; Emma almost liked her for it.

"You took your time in answering, young lady!" Mrs Appleby said disapprovingly. "We do not favour those who think to duck away from their responsibilities, by which I mean the rent payment, which is due today." She scowled at Emma, looking her up and down in an appraising way which was far different from Jairus Cuthbert's looks, but insulting, nonetheless.

"I have the money ready to pay. Five shillings and sixpence," Emma said with a flat smile as she reached into her pocket and withdrew the coins which she had retrieved from the hiding place earlier. She had known that surely someone would come for the rent and fearing what manner of a man it might be this time, she had been prepared. She simply thrust out her hand with the coins and continued to smile weakly at Mrs Appleby.

"First, we should like to come inside. We are very different agents from the last and we demand cleanliness in all rooms. You might be paying, young lady, but we won't put up with slovenliness. Cleanliness is next to Godliness after all," she said, and that simple sentence perfectly explained the appearance of piety, for the piety was real.

Vera Appleby reminded Emma of a ferret David had found as a small boy and begged his mother to keep, to no avail. She had a small face and her eyes were locked in a permanent squint, as if she couldn't see or she was deep in thought. It made her look furtive, just like the ferret had looked. Emma wondered idly if all landlords and landladies resembled rodents of some kind or another.

"Of course," Emma said, feeling a flush of pride as she showed the couple in. She was a clean person and had kept the place spotless even after her mother died. They had almost nothing, but what they had was clean.

Mrs Appleby walked in first, scurrying about the room and peering into every corner. Emma was pleased that she had taken their sheets into work at the big house and washed them with the others, for they were so obviously clean that she could have smiled in victory.

Mr Appleby followed, looking at Emma sideways. She realised what he was noting. As she had led them in, her prominent limp had been revealed. Emma did her best to suppress it, as she felt a strange sense of judgement from the couple as they saw her swinging gait, but she was only able to hide it so much, it was still very obvious.

"Well, how does it look?" he asked, turning to peer at David who was standing to attention at the side of his cleanly made mattress.

"Mmm. Clean," Mrs Appleby said, as if somehow disappointed to have nothing to disapprove of.

"I always keep our home clean, Mrs Appleby, just as my mother taught me to," Emma said and smiled.

But as Mrs Appleby turned slowly to look at her, it was clear that she was far from impressed. As impossible as it seemed, she managed to narrow her gaze even further, leaving Emma wondering if the woman could even see her at all.

"Young lady, pride is one of the seven deadly sins. If you were a God-fearing child, you would already know that."

"I am a God-fearing child. I take my brother to church every Sunday without fail. My mother brought us up right." Emma felt affronted by this woman. She was the sort of woman who could never be pleased.

Emma wondered then if it was impossible to win in the world. She would have been condemned by Mrs Appleby for being unclean, and now she was being condemned for disappointing her with her cleanliness. Emma had had just about enough of this world and the people who inhabited it.

Seeing the vexed expression on Mrs Appleby's face, Emma hurriedly changed the subject. "Are you the owners of the tenement? I had always thought Mr Cuthbert was and he did nothing to deny it."

"Oh, that wicked man!" Mrs Appleby hissed, and her husband gave an affirmative snort.

"Yes, he was a wicked man," Emma said without thinking.

"He was by no means the owner and my husband and I should never make such a grand pretence! This building is owned by a very fine gentleman indeed. I shan't tell you his name, for a girl like you would never have cause to know it. You will never meet him, after all." She continued to peer through the slits.

"He has never been here, I suppose?" Emma was suddenly curious.

"Goodness, no! Why would he?" Mrs Appleby looked as scandalised as a person who seemed to have no eyes could look. "It wouldn't be fitting at all for such a fine man to come here and deal with such people as live in this place. Not fitting at all!" As she ranted, Emma wondered if the impeccable Mrs Appleby considered herself among those same people. One not good enough to be noticed by the fine man who made his living off their misery, their need to spend five shillings and sixpence every week on such appalling rooms.

"Right, we shall take the money now. Hand it to my husband, for he is the man you answer to."

Emma handed the coins to the unsmiling Myron Appleby and wondered if he truly thought himself the one, of that pair, whom folk truly answered to.

CHAPTER 12

L ife had begun to even out somewhat, and Emma found herself gently lulled by the comforting predictability of it all. As the weeks went on and the warmer month of June made itself known, she began to feel a little more like her old self again.

Her attack wasn't forgotten, and the limp made sure it never would be, but her grief at her mother's passing had subsided somewhat, and she knew she could somehow keep things going. She was managing and she felt a little proud about that, regardless of the line often quoted by Mrs Apple by that pride was a deadly sin when she was within a couple of hundred yards of the market, Emma could hear a voice she recognised.

"Wi-ild rabbits, two a shilling! Penny a bunch of turnips." It was David and he sounded louder and more confident

than ever. He bellowed the words as if it was now second nature to do so, and Emma smiled to herself.

Her little brother had done a fair bit of growing up in the months since they'd lost their mother. He was no longer just a little boy who needed protection but a fine boy with a job, a purpose, and some pride in the responsibility he had taken on. It made her both proud and sad all at once, for she had wanted to keep that little boy innocent and content for as long as possible.

The market wasn't a bad place, but Emma knew that David would have heard things he'd never heard before. Swearing, lewd remarks, things he was too young to understand but things she had no doubt Spuddy would have cheerfully explained. It was a double-edged sword right enough.

With her cares and worries of the day threatening to hold her in their grip for goodness knew how long, Emma tried to clear her mind entirely. She tried to just feel the world around her; the slightly cooling air after so warm a day, the smell of baked bread fighting for pride of place amongst the horrors of the butcher's waste and the rotting food. It was just a way of being where she was without judging her circumstances. She didn't put the bread aroma over all the rest. It wasn't a contest, everything just was. This was the world. There was some measure of peace in this approach, but Emma wasn't foolish enough to think it would last.

When she was almost at the market, a smart looking young man passed her in the street. He had pale blond hair and blue eyes, and his clothes marked him out not as wealthy, exactly, but as someone who was managing a little better than the rest of them. He was older than her at perhaps twenty, and when he made a point of looking right at her, smiling before he gave a cheeky wink, Emma could hardly believe it. She looked back at him open-mouthed where once she might have smiled shyly and blushed a little. Where had that other Emma gone?

Seeing her expression and likely thinking it prudish outrage, the young man chuckled, touched the brim of his hat, and continued on his way. Emma stood still for a moment, her mind letting go of the tentative peace of the last few minutes as a little nausea rested in her throat.

In her heart, she knew his cheek to be nothing more, to be an innocent expression of a young man who saw a girl he liked the look of. But her nausea was dragging her back to that awful day, to the horror and the feelings of helplessness and humiliation.

Emma wondered if she would ever feel normal again. Just a few months before, when she had stared through the shop window at the pretty blue and pink bonnet, she surely would never have imagined a handsome young man's attention producing such a violent reaction. She would have been thrilled and, what's more, she would have let the little scene occupy her for days, adding to it, making it the story of her life to come. The young man would have been symbolic of her dreamed-of hero. He would have represented the life she wanted, the handsome man who would rescue her from the worries of life. But those worries back then had been simpler somehow. They had been the same worries that everybody else lived their lives alongside.

Now that her worries were bigger, her need to escape more pressing, Emma couldn't imagine the excitement of being rescued now.

Whichever way she looked at it, Emma felt doomed. She didn't want that kind of rescue, and it wasn't hers to be had even if she did. The whole moment had made her helplessness, in life, seem overwhelming and she realised that she now, without a doubt, felt utterly without hope. There was a part of her, a large part, which simply wanted to lay down on the dirty road right where she was and simply stay there until it was all over. She wanted to give up, to admit that this life had defeated her before she was even sixteen-years-old.

But then she heard his voice again, *"Wi-ild rabbits, two a shilling! Penny a bunch of turnips,"* and she knew she had to keep going. If she laid down now and let go of this dreadful existence, what would become of David? Into whose hands would he fall, and what would those hands teach that precious boy about the world?

"Eye-eye! Here comes the Duchess!" Spuddy called out humorously as she approached. "And what sort of day have you had up at the big house, Duchess?" He grinned, that solitary tooth an offence to the eye.

"A day much the same as any other, Spuddy," she said and managed to both laugh and smile. But in her mind, in her heart, it was some other girl who responded. It was some other girl who went on to make inconsequential conversation with the garrulous costermonger in the heart of the Clerkenwell market.

The real Emma had withdrawn from life, had turned her back on it all. There was nobody to notice, to realise it, and yet it was the case. Emma had silently given up.

CHAPTER 13

Martha Jones had been quiet for the entire work day. Emma had never seen her ordinary mood of complaint and strident instruction so displaced before. It wasn't only Emma who'd noticed, for she had witnessed more than one curious glance being exchanged between the other maids, scullery maids, and even the footmen. What was most alarming, though, was most of these quiet exchanges also included a quick glance towards Emma herself, as if she was involved in the strange happenings.

"Emma. I know I have never asked before, but now I feel I must. What happened, the day you came to us battered and bruised?" Martha asked when the two of them were finally alone in the yard where Emma was hanging the laundry.

"You must know, Mrs Jones?" Emma said, completely thrown by the question.

It was September now, still warm, but the good drying days were soon going to come to an end. Emma had been grateful for the cooler air.

Martha only let out a small sigh of confirmation in reply. When Emma turned to look at her, the poor woman looked awful.

"My landlord, a man my mother had protected me from for so long. He saw me as some temptress, some harlot laughing at him in pride. I never did anything of the sort, Martha, you have to believe me! When I tried paying the rent, he threw me across his room."

"The one who was murdered in the tavern?"

"Yes, Jairus Cuthbert. When I'd heard he lay dead in the tavern... I gave sixpence to a peeler so that I might look down on his body and be sure he was gone. There, now you know what a truly awful person I am." She looked down, wondering why no tears would come when she felt so utterly defeated. Emma could feel something foreboding hanging in the air, and knew there was no point in trying to soften any of the story, even in ways that might benefit her.

"I don't blame you for that," Martha said sadly. "I don't blame you for any of it. You're not an awful person, Emma. You're a person to whom life has been so dreadfully cruel." Martha's eyes filled with tears. "But something has happened, Emma. Or rather, someone has said something."

"Said something?" Emma wasn't sure why Martha was stringing this out, she was never one to mince words usually.

"Oh, my poor dear child," Martha said as a solitary tear tracked its way down her cheek. "The mistress of the house has expressed her desire that her staff be all fit and presentable... and able." Emma felt the sinking feeling intensify. "And she has been informed that she has... a cripple working in her house, and she would not have that."

"A cripple!" Emma had to fight not to raise her voice too loudly as to draw unwanted attention. "Martha, I am not a cripple! I might limp, but I can still get around just fine. I do all my work on time, I... I..." Emma felt at a loss for words.

"I know you aren't Emma, and I know you work so hard, but... She demanded that I dismiss you this very day. She says she does not want such decrepitness in her house." Martha hurriedly dashed her tears away as if she couldn't do what must be done whilst in so emotional a state. "I really am sorrier than I could ever tell you."

"But... That isn't fair! Just because I limp, they're going kick me out onto the street all of a sudden?" Emma's face burnt with fear and anger.

"They do not think as we do, Emma. They do not see the struggles of people all around them. Their only concern is to have those same people see to their every need, their every whim, without complaint. That is who they are."

"Surely, that is where the wrong in this world truly lives!" Emma was angry and afraid. How could this be happening? How could any of it be happening when all she'd ever tried to do was live in this world and do right day after day?

"You have to look to the future now. You have to make a plan and dwelling on the heartlessness of those who truly believe they are our betters won't help you. It'll drain you. It'll take your last ounce of strength; injustice always does."

"I'm sunk, Mrs Jones. I am sunk with no hope for survival."

"The Lord will provide, my child. I'm sorry, it's the only advice I can give to you." Finally, Martha pulled Emma into her arms.

It was a strange feeling. Emma clung to Martha, knowing that this would be the last day the two of them would be together. This would be that one and only moment of human kindness and Emma didn't ever want to let go.

In the end, Martha had given her a cup of strong, sweet tea in the kitchen and packed a bag with as much food as she could reasonably give her without the minor theft coming to light. And then, when the time came for her to go, Martha gave her the last of her wages. Emma looked down at the few shillings in her hand and felt as if her life were over.

"And take this," Martha said, holding back her tears as she pressed yet more coins into her hand. "It's not much, but it should pay for the next two weeks rent."

Emma looked into her hand again and saw that Martha had given her ten shillings. The kindness was almost too much to bear, and Emma began to break down. She couldn't speak, not even to thank Martha for giving her the coins when she undoubtedly had need of them herself.

"It's time, Emma," Martha said and tried to straighten her own spine before walking her to the servants' door for the last time.

As Emma walked slowly through the streets, her tears streamed down her face. She cried without a sound but still drew the odd glance from people passing her. However, nobody stopped. Nobody asked her what was wrong or if they could help. She hadn't expected anything else, of course, for this was the world she lived in. Hard lives made people hard themselves, immune to the suffering of others, their empathy dissolved with their own fading fortunes. But Emma wasn't hard, despite everything that had happened to her.

Making no attempt to dry her face, Emma's attention was drawn to the shop window she and her mother had looked through all those months before. She knew what drew her; the need to know if somebody else had bought the blue and pink bonnet. She wanted to know that the silly dream was gone now, the bonnet already on the head of another young woman, one whose life was better than her own. But the bonnet was still there.

Emma stood as still as a statue in front of the window and stared at the bonnet. She remembered her dreams on that day, and better still, remembered just how and when those dreams had been smashed to pieces. She remembered the smart young man who had winked at her in the market and made her feel so humiliated once again. How she had turned from the idea of rescue. Now, however, Emma would have given anything for such a rescue, whatever the cost. She would give anything for a fine man to lean on, to be cherished by. A man who would help her through the worst of times and understand the horror of what had brought her so low. A man who would know that she had not been anything other than an innocent bystander watching her own awful life unfolding, and powerless to do anything about it.

Emma knew that she had truly lost everything now. Even hopes and dreams were not to be hers for she was wise enough now to know that such fairy tales did not happen to young women in her circumstances. Jairus Cuthbert had taken everything from her in just a matter of moments, right down to her right to dream.

Emma turned away from the window and stared out across the street. She never wanted to see that bonnet ever again, nor did she ever want to think about it. The bag of food Martha had given her was weighing heavy in her hands and she knew she just had to keep moving. She just had to get through this day, and when the next day arrived, she just had to get through that one too.

Martha had been kind, but she would be the only one. On this, Emma Mason's sixteenth birthday, her only gift was to be a few shillings and a bag of food to keep her and David alive for a matter of days. In the end, perhaps that was a more fitting gift than a beautiful blue and pink bonnet with its lacy trim and all the silent hopes it had once represented.

CHAPTER 14

I t took exactly two days for the gossip to make its way from the big house to the tenements of Clerkenwell. Two days in which Emma had hobbled blindly, dazed, confused, and terrified. David had known there was something wrong when Emma did not set off for work the morning after she had been dismissed.

"Aren't you working today, Emma?" he'd asked, his big blue eyes full of worry.

"Not today, David," she'd replied, not knowing what to tell him. A part of her had wanted to stay silent. If she did not give voice to all that had happened, perhaps there was a slim hope that it had never happened at all. She didn't want to make it real, not yet.

"Are you sick?" he asked, his fearful face telling her that he was already thinking of the scarlet fever and how it had so quickly taken their mother.

"No, no, I'm not sick." She wanted to reassure him of that much at least. "Now, get along with you, Spuddy will be waiting."

The next day had followed with the same conversation and Emma knew that she would soon have to tell David everything. She would have to strip him of his innocence and have him know at last what a dreadful place the world could be. But before she had a chance to work out what she would say, the opportunity was stolen from her by Myron and Vera Appleby.

Shortly after David had returned from a long day's work with the costermonger, there came a loud knock at the door. Before Emma had time to cross the room, it was knocked on again, and she could hear the whining tones of Vera Appleby outside. What could she possibly want? She had paid the rent on Friday as always.

"Mrs Appleby?" Emma said timidly when she opened the door a crack. "Whatever is the matter?"

Without waiting to be asked, Mrs Appleby pushed her way into the room. It wasn't until she was fully inside that Emma realised Mr Appleby had walked in behind her. She looked at him, her face a picture of confusion. There was no confusion on Myron Appleby's face, however, just the purest and most unmistakable disgust. Emma's palms began to perspire and David, already across the room, began to back instinctively into the corner by his little bed.

"Well, let's have a look at you," Mrs Appleby said, and Emma stared at her, her mouth open. "You're obviously not shy, so let's have a look at you."

"I don't know what you mean, Mrs Appleby," Emma said, feeling her entire body beginning to shake.

"She doesn't look like a killer, Vera..." Myron Appleby said softly to his wife.

"A killer? What are you talking about?" Emma started to panic.

"The wolf shall be dressed in sheep's clothing." Vera said to her husband before turning on Emma. "We knew that the previous landlord wasn't always the most pleasant to you, little Miss. But murder is a sin most foul and severe. You have sinned against God, Emma Mason, what do you have to say about that?"

"I, as everyone has, have sinned, Mrs Appleby. I have sinned and been sinned against. But I can promise you, I would never even attempt to murder someone!"

"We heard about you going to gloat over the body!" Vera Appleby screeched. Her ferret-like face was twitching, her eyes narrowed to slits.

"People are talking, Miss Mason." Myron said, staying much more level-headed. "And it doesn't look the best, now does it?"

Tears of shame and injustice began to roll from Emma's eyes. "I... I didn't kill him, I swear. I was told you could pay the police to see the body. Jairus Cuthbert was the man who assaulted me, left me with this limp, and not even two weeks after my mother's death! It was wrong, I know that, I see that now. But I just wanted to look on the man who has taken everything from me. I just went and looked, I had nothing to do with his death. Ask anyone!"

"And you think we are so stupid as to believe that, do you?" Vera somehow found a way to look even more disgusted. "Look at you. God has punished you for your immoral thoughts and actions. I wouldn't be surprised if you were the one to drive Jairus into action." She turned to her husband, who was staring down at the floor. "I wouldn't be surprised if this girl never paid rent ever, at least, not in the moral way!"

"That just isn't true, Mrs Appleby. What an awful thing to say." Emma's tears were now falling faster than she could dry them. "Now, this is my home and I demand that you leave it immediately. I pay rent here and always on time. You can't just barge in and attack me."

"This most certainly is *not* your home, not anymore, young lady." Vera said triumphantly. "You must leave immediately."

"But my rent is paid. My rent is paid until Friday!"

"Go and tell it to somebody who cares, Emma Mason." Vera said.

Myron intervened. "Dear, she can at least have until tomorrow morning." He glanced at Emma in apology and shame. "To make sure she has time to collect all her wretched things, and leave nothing behind." The second sentence sounded foreign and unconvincing in Myron's mouth, but his attempt to appeal to his wife worked.

Vera nodded her head definitively. "Tomorrow morning then. And when all of Clerkenwell knows you for what you are, there will not be a person out there who will take pity on you. You are an offence to God and man and the only place you're fit to live in is the workhouse. You will be ready to leave tomorrow morning, or I will cast you out into the street without any of your belongings, which shall all be burnt. Come, Mr Appleby, we have already spent too much time in the lowest of all company. Some sinners can't be reached, and she is just one of them," Mrs Appleby finished, shaking her head and scowling at Emma once more before turning to leave the room. Myron, following his wife, turned to look back at Emma one last time. For a moment it seemed like he would speak, but he said nothing. He just sighed, before turning and gently closing the door behind him.

"Don't cry, Emma," David said half an hour later when Emma was still sobbing. She had sat on her mattress, so utterly dejected that she didn't know what move to make next.

110

"Oh David, my dear boy, I'm so sorry. I'm so, so sorry," Emma said.

"It's not your fault, Emma. Mr Cuthbert was the one to blame. Mr Cuthbert was the one who hurt you. I hate him! I hate him and I'm glad he's dead!" David said furiously.

"David, I know you don't understand how these things happen and I can't bring myself to tell you."

"You're always trying to protect me, and you never let me protect you." David looked as if he was on the verge of tears.

"Well, I haven't done much good at protecting you, have I? I haven't protected you from the awfulness of this world and now I can't even keep a roof over your head. It's all too much, David. I just don't know what to do." David kneeled on the mattress beside her and wrapped his thin arms around her neck. He held on tightly and she could feel his little body shaking with silent sobs.

Childhood was most certainly over for Emma Mason, but she had never imagined the awfulness of realising that it was also over for David. She had no idea what they would do or where they would go. Even if the dreadful Vera Appleby had allowed them to stay until Friday, she doubted things would have been any clearer.

Even though she had the few coins that Martha Jones had given her, she knew it would be pointless now to pay it in rent in some other tenement building. It would cover no more than a few days, two weeks at the most, and then they would simply be thrown out again only this time they would not have a penny to their names. They would just have to find somewhere safe, somewhere dry at least, and hold onto that little bit of money so that they could at least buy food for a while. But then what? When that money ran out, what would they do? The pittance that David earned with Spuddy every day would hardly feed them and would certainly not put a roof over their heads, however lowly that roof might be.

She knew her only alternative to a life on the streets was the workhouse, but she knew that once inside neither one of them would ever make their way out again.

Emma realised then that there wasn't a step she could make in this world that would be right. David would be forced to work harder than any boy of ten should, the fun and chatter of the marketplace and Spuddy ripped from him. But how could she keep them both safe without anywhere for them to rest their heads?

"We'd better get some sleep, Emma. We'd better get some sleep whilst we still have a bed and somewhere dry. If we are awake all night, tomorrow will seem so much worse," David said, his voice breaking with fear and emotion.

"You are such a sensible boy, David. Perhaps I haven't given you much credit for knowing how the world really works. I suppose I just didn't want you to know it, I didn't want you to see it. I wanted you to be a child for as long as possible, even in this awful place where so many childhoods are lost before they begin. I'm so, so sorry. I don't know what to do, David, and I am so, so sorry."

CHAPTER 15

On that first night, Emma and David huddled for warmth in the alleyway which ran between the baker's shop and the end of a long tenement building. It was far away from the smells of the butcher's shop and there was a little warmth emanating from the old brick from the ovens which ran through the night. Of course, such a warm place was popular, and Emma was a little dismayed to discover just how many people came there to sleep after dark.

As the alley began to become a little more populated, Emma felt a little less alone. There were a couple of kindly faces, both women, who made a fuss of David and tried to reassure Emma they would be safe as long as they remained vigilant. Emma was left wondering how a person might get a night's sleep whilst simultaneously remaining vigilant, but she kept her question to herself. As the night went on, however, those who had finished in the tavern came to settle down and Emma realised that sleep, from now on, would have to be something she got in the early part of the evening.

"Try to get some sleep, David. You don't want to be falling asleep with Spuddy tomorrow." Emma pulled David tighter to her, wrapping her shawl around him too. It was cold enough now and it was only September. What on earth would it be like to sleep outside in the depths of a cold winter? She couldn't think about it, even though she knew she must.

When Emma and David had quit their little room early on the first morning of their homelessness, Emma had folded all their possessions and placed them together, tying them inside an old heavy woollen shawl that once belonged to her mother. She had tied the corners together like a handle so that she might carry their few things with ease, regardless of her limp. However, without four walls, the shawl was a horrible reminder of just how little they had in the world.

Emma still had the few shillings that Martha had given her. She had been shrewd enough to divide them and put a few coins in each stocking, laying them flat beneath the soles of her feet before putting her boots back on. She kept a little ready money in her pocket, knowing that if they were robbed, their attacker would be unlikely to imagine she hid most of her money beneath her feet.

On the first night in the alleyway, Emma had almost decided that she would spend half their money on a room. She had it in mind to scour the area for work of any kind, but she immediately began to wonder what would happen if she found no such employment. She would have wasted the money that they needed for food. Emma had never felt more trapped in her life, stuck exactly where she was for fear of making the wrong choices.

Her thoughts kept her awake the better part of that first night, and she realised that, by the time morning came, she had slept for little more than half an hour. The sun came up brightly that morning and yet it was an offence to her eyes. It made the Clerkenwell streets look somehow more appealing and yet, as a woman who had spent her night sleeping in them, she knew that they were anything but. At least it hadn't rained, that was something. Surely, if it rained the alleyway would be no good to anybody and they would be forced to search for a doorway to shelter in and hope that the peelers did not come to move them along.

Emma could already feel the spiral of helplessness. A person without a home stood little chance of getting a job and a person without a job stood little chance of getting a home. It was that very situation that so many people fought to keep themselves safe from day after day, living and working in poverty and struggling their way through lives which had no meaning beyond survival. But she had fallen into the pit, she had tripped over her own life and was now tumbling deeper and deeper, faster and faster, into hopelessness.

"I'd better go and find Spuddy, Emma," David said, twisting in her arms to look up at her, his eyelids puffy from lack of sleep and his smooth skin a little grey with fatigue and worry.

"All right, I'll walk with you," she said, rising awkwardly to her feet and realising just how much her body ached from lack of sleep and a night spent sitting on the cold ground leaning against a wall, on top of the dull ache that was ever present in her hip.

She gathered their bits and pieces together, making sure that she had everything tucked neatly into her mother's woollen shawl. Turning to nod her thanks at the two women who had made them feel just a little safer throughout the night, Emma realised just how desperate and unwell they looked. Each had sallow skin and sunken eyes, prominent cheekbones and the inevitable appearance of being unkempt which declared a person's homelessness more loudly than words ever could.

Emma and David made their way out of the alleyway, Emma holding tightly to David's hand and David, for once, not objecting. He was tired and just as hopeless as she was, Emma was sure of that, and he allowed her to hold onto his hand all the way to the Clerkenwell market.

"Where is he, Emma? Where's Spuddy?" David asked, looking up at his sister as if she might by some miracle have the answer to his question.

"I don't know. His cart's normally here, isn't it?" It was her turn to ask a pointless question now. "Look, just wait here for a moment and I'll go and ask somebody."

Emma gave David the shawl filled with their belongings and wandered alone into the market to find out if anybody there had seen Spuddy. Seeing one of the men who were often found enjoying a laugh and a joke with the costermonger, Emma hurried up to him.

"Well, if you ain't the Duchess!" the man said and smiled, an entirely toothless smile which was warm and friendly, nonetheless. However, she wished that Spuddy had never given her such a nickname for now it felt like a mockery, even if the poor man uttering it most certainly didn't mean it as such. "I expect you're looking for Spuddy," he went on, wincing.

"I am, do you know where he is? My brother works for him, you see," she said, adding the last uselessly for the man could be in no doubt whatsoever that little David Mason was the costermonger's sidekick.

"Unfortunately, I do know where he is, Duchess. Got himself into a spot of bother, he did, and the peelers have got him." The man shrugged, showing as much care as anybody in their world was able to spare for another.

"But when will he be back?" Emma asked, feeling the ground shift beneath her feet once more; would this misery never end?

"Might be a while, Duchess. He'd had a few too many last night, see, and he fell back into his old ways."

"What do you mean?"

"I mean one ale over the top and he was taken right back to his childhood, wasn't he! Tried to pick a toff's pocket on his way home. Unfortunately for him, the toff was a magistrate's nephew and the peelers were there in a heartbeat. Old Spuddy tried to apologise, tried to say it was the drink and nothing more as he handed the man's purse back, but the toff would hear none of it. Stood there squawking and squeaking until the peelers put the manacles on him and carted him off."

"Oh, my goodness, poor Spuddy." Emma felt miserable, her mother had always warned them about stealing, but she knew that her worries were more for herself and David than for the costermonger. It made her feel almost inhuman. She was already becoming the sort of person whose cares were so great that she couldn't spare the room for somebody else's misfortunes. Was her humanity to be stripped from her too?

"But when will he be back?" she asked again.

"It will be a while, Duchess. Just be glad a bit of drunken thieving isn't a deporting or hanging offence these days.

Oh, but he'll do a spell in the prison, won't he? Can't be trying to pinch a toff's purse and get off scot free. I reckon that brother of yours will need to be looking for another job."

"Do you know of any? Jobs, I mean. For either my brother or me," Emma said and her cheeks flushed when the man allowed his gaze to shift momentarily to her left leg which at that moment was bracing her at a slightly odd angle.

"There's nothing going around here that I know of, I'm sorry. But maybe have the boy wander about the market for the day and see what he can find. If he hovers about long enough and keeps asking folk, somebody will give into him in the end, trust me."

"And do you think there would be anything for me?"

"I don't know, love," he said, and she was glad he seemed to have dropped the *Duchess*. "Maybe some workhouses might take you? Ones that have you sit most of the time." He went on, and she could see the pity in his eyes. "Look, let the boy wander about for the day and see what he can find. As for yourself, try some of the middling houses on the edge of Clerkenwell. You might find somebody there who is in want of a bit of domestic help but not so fussy about references and the like. Don't worry about him, I'll keep an eye out," the man smiled at her and nodded.

"Thank you. Thank you very much," Emma said, instinctively knowing that this man was by no means the watchful guardian that Spuddy had been. His heart was in the right place, but she very much doubted that his concentration would be up to it. Still, what choice did she have?

She made her way back to David and took the shawl from him. Explaining what he must do, she beseeched him to behave himself, to be on the lookout for anybody who might seek to either harm him or lead him astray.

"I know what I'm doing, Emma," David said a little sharply, something which she immediately put down to a lack of sleep. "I've worked in this market for a long time and I wish you'd stop treating me like a baby. I know more about this market than you do, so just leave me to it."

"All right, David," she said gently, blinking fast to stop sudden tears from falling.

"Sorry," he said, immediately softening and turning back into the angel-faced little boy she loved so much. He wrapped his arms around her, burying his little face into her chest and holding back tears of his own. "I shouldn't have been mean."

"You're not mean, David, you're just tired and afraid the same as I am. And you're right, you're not a baby and it won't help either of us now if I keep treating you like one. I trust you to know what you're doing, and I love you." She kissed the top of his head. Part of her wanted to warn him. To tell him not to steal, but he wouldn't, she knew that.

"And I love you too," he said, freeing himself from her arms and hastily wiping his tears away before anybody in the market might see them.

CHAPTER 16

David waited for his sister to disappear from sight before walking to the very edge of the market, the opposite end from where he ordinarily worked with Spuddy. He didn't want to think about Spuddy now, flopped in some cell whilst he waited to go before the Magistrate. David liked Spuddy and had even wished he was his father once or twice.

He had no memory of his own father, or at least nothing very firm. Benedict Mason was nothing more than a vague outline to him. A great bear of a man whom David remembered looking down at him and smiling. Beyond that, his greater and more distinct memories were of a mother who would never talk about her husband and so, having last seen the man when he was just four-years-old, David had let go of him with much more ease than his sister. He knew that Emma still loved their father and that she silently prayed for him to return one day. But as far as

David could see, fathers who wandered off surely didn't wander back. Why would they?

David knew where he was going, and it had nothing to do with wandering from stall to stall in the market begging for work. For as long as he'd worked for Spuddy, David had seen boys his own age doing just the same thing and he had yet to see any of them be successful. Why would he waste his day doing that when he already knew that there was more of a sure thing to be found on the outer edges?

Working for Spuddy these last months had meant that David knew the market as well as anybody, including the little industries which conducted themselves in the shadows beyond. He let his hands rest in his pocket and wandered along looking nonchalant and inconspicuous. From what he'd seen, that was the very best way to go about things. He was looking for somebody in particular, a boy he had watched time and time again. David knew that he himself must be good for the boy had never once turned to look at him; he probably never knew that David was watching him so closely.

When he got to the end of the market, he moved to lean against the wall of an abandoned building, its windows boarded, and its door nailed shut. He knew it was a place where the homeless went when they could get in, but it was also a place that had become popular with the patrolling peelers. They would take great delight in turfing people out of that place and into the cold and unforgiving night. It was such a pointless prospect that he had never considered mentioning it to his sister; he didn't want to get her hopes up.

Finally, David saw exactly who he was looking for. The boy was a little older than him, perhaps fourteen or fifteen, and he was taller, leaner, and much more impressive. But at the same time, he blended in. He had his hands thrust into his pocket and walked along with a nonchalant air. There was nothing to make him stand out from anybody else in the Clerkenwell streets. It was the style that David had mimicked, adopted as his own. And David admired the older boy, he had done so for some time. The boy worked without ever once being suspected. There were adults all around them, sharp adults like Spuddy and his friends, but none of them sharp enough to see what David had seen. And when he'd first seen it, it had been so quick that he had spent the rest of the day wondering if he'd really seen it at all.

David had been so caught up in it all, that he'd returned some days later and watched again, training his eye and his concentration to a fine point until he really did see what he thought he'd seen all along. The boy had picked the pocket of a well-to-do man who had walked through the market and was heading away. In no time at all, the boy had removed the contents of the little purse and discarded it, stowing the money in his pocket and all without a single person, barring David, having seen what he'd done. All without breaking his stride and all without looking at all suspicious. David had been so impressed, so enthralled, that he had returned again and again to watch the older boy in action.

As he leaned against the wall, his hands still in his pockets as he mimicked the older boy's style, David watched as yet another well-to-do man was relieved of his purse. He knew it was wrong, for his mother had always told him that stealing was the worst thing, something he must never do. At the same time, however, he recognised the skill, the elegance. The older boy was a master of his craft and, despite the immorality, there must surely be some merit in having the lightness of touch not to mention the sheer guts to carry it out.

The boy surreptitiously ditched the purse in a pile of rotting rubbish in the gutter and continued to walk without anybody but David having realised what had happened. No doubt the man would soon notice that his purse was gone, but likely not until he looked for it again. He might suspect he'd been relieved of his coins somewhere near the market, or he might not. There might be any number of places he would suspect between where he was now and home, and therein lay the beauty, as far as David could see. If a boy had skills, he could survive. And why should a boy not survive? Why should a boy and his sister who had never done anybody any wrong not survive? If this was what it took, then this was what it took. It wasn't in David's sphere of understanding to pull it apart, to analyse it and look at it from every angle. He'd seen something that might help them that was as much as he needed to understand.

"I'm starting to think you want to marry me," the boy changed direction so suddenly and so smoothly that David could do no more than let his mouth open and close like a fish without any sound coming out whatsoever. "Well, what do you think? Shall we go and speak to the vicar and see if he'll make room for us at the alter this afternoon?" The boy began to chuckle, and David felt his cheeks flush with embarrassment.

The boy was only a few years older, but he might just as well have been a fully-grown man. Without knowing anything more about him, David was already certain that he had twice the intelligence of Spuddy and ten times the life experience.

"I'm sorry, I didn't mean to," David said, not knowing what else to say.

"You didn't mean to watch me?" The boy was smiling but it wasn't an unpleasant smile; David was perturbed but he certainly didn't feel afraid.

"It's all right, nobody else saw you," David said, hoping to curry favour.

"I know nobody else saw me. Nobody ever sees me. Apart from you, of course. Young master eagle-eyes you are, aren't you?" The boy's eyes were a very pale blue and yet his face was dark. His skin would have been olive in colour had it not been for that thin sheen of dirt which made it look rather more grey. His eyes looked almost peculiar sitting there in such dark surroundings. "The look on your face! Did you really think I hadn't seen you all the times you made your way here to have a good gander?"

"I wasn't going to tell, honest." David suddenly felt exposed, foolish. "I just wanted to learn, I just wanted to do what you can do. Not that I'd do it here. I mean I wouldn't step on your toes," David said, talking fast and beginning to feel a little excited; the boy was smiling at him thoughtfully.

"There's plenty of places; pickings for all, as they say," the boy chuckled again and leaned against the building next to him, his face turned to study David. "I suppose you'll be needing it now since Spuddy went down," he went on, surprising David entirely.

"How did you know that…?"

"That you used to work for Spuddy? I saw you the very first day you saw me, mate. You're not too bad at it; you creep around enough that most folk wouldn't notice you, but I did. Anyway, I followed you back to the costermonger I did, and saw that you were Spuddy's sidekick. So, what are you going to do now?"

"Well, it doesn't look like Spuddy will be coming back for a while, so I need to make some money. Me and my sister got thrown out of our lodgings, you see. We slept in an alleyway last night but it ain't right," he went on, adopting the slightly rougher speech of his new friend. "She needs to sleep somewhere warm and I'll do anything to look after her. *Anything,*" he added and raised his little eyebrows significantly.

"I reckon you would too!" the boy said and grinned at him. "And I reckon you'd do it a treat! You look like a bleedin' angel or an altar boy. Nobody would suspect you, would they?"

"Then you think I'd be able to do it? Will you help me?" David asked, growing in confidence and determined not to back down now.

"I reckon I could help you, but we need to go and see somebody first."

"See somebody? But who?" David asked, feeling the first flutter of consternation.

"Well, I don't just work on my own, do I? There's plenty of us."

"But who do I have to see?"

"Mr Griswold is who you'd have to see, mate. He runs the whole thing."

"What whole thing? What do you mean?"

"He's the one who organises us all, teaches us the trade, tells us where to go and how to avoid being picked up by the peelers. Takes a cut, mind you, but it's worth it."

"How much of a cut does he take?" David asked, beginning to think that it might be better for him to work alone.

"You won't get a better deal anywhere. Somewhere to live, somewhere to sleep. And that's from the very first day, mind you. He's a rum 'un, all right, but he looks after us all in his own way."

"So, we'd have somewhere to sleep? Tonight?" David asked, already wondering how he would present all of this to his sister; the same sister who was always worried he would get himself into trouble.

"If Mr Griswold likes the look of you, yes."

"And my sister too? I mean, she wouldn't be able to do this. She's got a bad leg. Some monster of a man hurt her and left his mark." he said, neglecting to mention the fact that she would never, ever have agreed to steal from anybody.

"Well, we'd have to see what Mr Griswold says about that. He'd need to see the both of you. Where's your sister now?"

"She's looking for work."

"Well, if she's got the gait of a cripple, I think the chances of finding work are pretty slim," he said and laughed. "So, when you find her, the two of you can wait for me here. I'll go back and have a word with Mr Griswold now and see what he thinks to it all and then, if he does want to see you both, you can come with me, can't you?"

"Yes, all right," David said and nodded vigorously.

"All right then, what's your name?"

"David Mason, and my sister is Emma."

"Well I'm Freddie Quince," he said and stuck his hand out as if the two of them had just agreed on some gentlemanly bit of business. "I'll be back here before the market closes, all right?"

"All right," David said and watched him walk away.

CHAPTER 17

D avid was waiting for her when she returned to the market. It had been such a long day and Emma was already tired of carrying all their worldly possessions in the shawl. It wasn't just the weight, nor the fact that the parcel was cumbersome, but rather that she had felt every person she had spoken to that day looking at her and judging her, sometimes consciously, sometimes not. Everyone instantly assessed her as soon as they saw her walk, the exaggerated shifting of weight. As such, nobody had wanted her. Who would want to hire a crippled girl who was clearly homeless? And she could see how most looked at her, imagining that her homelessness was her own fault. What a sickening place this world was, so filled with judgement and so lacking in kindness.

"Emma, I have somewhere for us to stay. Well, I think I do, but we have to speak to Mr Griswold," David said excitedly, his big blue eyes wide and full of hope.

"Who is Mr Griswold? Have you found a job? You clever boy, what will you be doing?" Emma could hardly believe it. Could things finally be taking a turn for the better?

"I don't know if I've found a real job yet, but I might have. I'd be working with other boys, you see, and if Mr Griswold likes us, we'll have somewhere to live too. Freddie said it ain't so fancy, but it's warm and dry and you'll have somewhere safe to sleep."

"Isn't, David, not ain't," Emma said, wondering just who David had spent the day with. "And who is Freddie?"

"He's an older boy, we've got to go meet him at the other end of the market in a few minutes. Freddie will take us to see Mr Griswold and see if I can get some work and we can live there with them." David had already begun to look crestfallen as if he knew that his sister was about to disapprove.

"What sort of work, David?" Emma asked, feeling the old dejection return, all her hopes squashed.

"I know we're not supposed to steal, Emma, I know it's wrong, but so are a lot of other things. Firing a good worker just because of a crippled leg is wrong, isn't it? And throwing two children out into the street without any hope of finding somewhere safe is wrong too, isn't it? And all these wrong things are done by adults, aren't they? Why should children be so good all the time when nobody else is? When none of the adults are? They made life this way for us, Emma. They did this," David said, and tears began to roll down his cheeks. "And if it's a choice between starving to death and having to steal for a living, then I'm going to steal. I've been watching Freddie for a long time and he's really good at it, and I know I could be too." He looked furious and beseeching all at once.

"I know life isn't fair, David," Emma said, hardly able to believe how her little brother's words had struck her. After all, there wasn't a single thing that he'd said that was wrong, she knew that. What she hadn't realised, however, was just how much he had perceived of the world around him and how he had neatly and cleanly been able to separate true badness from desperate need. He had seen the world of adults for what they were, and he had quite rightly judged that the blame for everything the brother and sister were suffering lay with those same adults. "And you're right, everything you said, David. You are a clever boy, so much smarter than I ever gave you credit for. But I can't bear the idea of you being caught, taken away by the peelers and put into prison or sent to the gallows. I am supposed to be looking after you."

"No, we are supposed to be looking after each other. I couldn't save you from Mr Cuthbert, but maybe I can save you from living in the alley. We have to look out for each other."

"I don't know what to say to you, David," Emma said and sighed deeply.

"Then say you'll come with me to meet Freddie. There's no work here, not for me, not for you. If we stay out here, we'll be out here forever. You will end up like one of those two old crones who looked after us last night, won't you? That's if you live that long. We've tried to be good, haven't we? But I don't think we can be good any longer and stay alive. And I want to stay alive, Emma. I want to stay alive," he said and began to cry in earnest.

Emma scooped him into her arms and held him tightly, running her hand over his curly mop of blond hair and soothing him as best she could.

"Come along then, let me meet this Freddie," Emma said, feeling her heart sink to her stomach and knowing that she really didn't have an option.

The garret was at the very top of a large terraced house just south of Farringdon. It had taken them almost half an hour to walk there from Clerkenwell, largely because Emma was exhausted and could hardly keep up with the boys. Freddie Quince was around her age, she thought, perhaps a little younger, and of a type so common in the poorer parts of London. She realised immediately that it was unlikely he had even been privileged enough to grow up as she and David had, with a loving parent and at least a few years in which to be a child. He was a fast talking grifter, his cheeky smile undoubtedly hiding all the pain of his past. However, as sorry for him as she was, Emma knew that she would never trust Freddie Quince as far as she could throw him.

"There are a lot of stairs, Emma," Freddie said with a grin when they were at the very bottom. "We'll go slowly," he chuckled, trying to be friendly, but it didn't make Emma feel any better. Instead, she felt afraid. Every step she took felt like a step further towards the unknown and she didn't like it one little bit.

By the time they reached the top of the staircase, Emma was out of breath. The stairs had been hard on her hip, and the dull ache had invaded her entire leg. She paused at the very top, trying to steady her breath so that she wouldn't look afraid when she was finally presented to Mr Griswold. Whoever he was, Emma knew already that he couldn't possibly be a good man.

"Come in, come in, don't just stand there at the top of the stairs, I don't bite," the voice was deep but jovial, the accent a curious attempt at a cultured tone. It seemed ridiculous, almost like an actor in a play, but somehow it made her feel less afraid.

"This is Emma and David Mason, Mr Griswold, them as I was telling you about before," Freddie said, looking up at the older man as if waiting for his approval. It reminded her of a dog peering hopefully up at his master.

"Well, hello, Emma and David Mason. Looks like the two of you have fallen on some rather rotten times," and there it was again, that attempt at cultured tone when the man looked ragged and unkempt.

Mr Griswold was tall and thin, his arms and legs reminding Emma of the summer spiders, the ones with the round body and impossibly thin legs. He had a long beard that came down to a ragged point, dark skin, dark eyes, and matted dark hair. Emma tried to smile at him, all the while holding back a very obvious grimace.

"If I work with you, Mr Griswold, will my sister be allowed to stay here? She needs to be in the warm, you see, and I'll do anything, anything at all." David surprised her with his confident tone; it was the tone he had learned from Spuddy. Right there and then, Emma would have given anything to see Spuddy's face again, his one-toothed grin.

"That's a fine little brother you have there, Miss Emma. I hope you're proud of him, my dear," Mr Griswold stared right into her face.

"I am very proud of him, Mr Griswold. But I'm also afraid for him," she said, pleased that her voice didn't tremble as her hands did behind her back. "I wouldn't want to see him in trouble with the peelers, sir," she added the last in the hope that he would not think she was disrespecting him. They needed somewhere to stay, they needed this desperately even as it was the very last thing she wanted in the world.

"Let me put your mind at rest, Miss Emma. My boys very rarely get caught by the peelers and do you know why?" he said, drawing a breath and ready to continue, not expecting an answer to his question. "Because I train them right, my dear. They are the best of the best in London, maybe even in all of England. Little David here won't be sent out without a clue, I can assure you. You see, it serves me well to have a well-trained boy, one who I've spent a little time on, a little effort on. It's no good to me if he gets pinched the first time he's let loose on Farringdon market or Blackfriars market, is it? No, I train them right."

"I see." Emma nodded, hardly able to believe that such skulduggery gave her some comfort.

"And you will have somewhere to stay too, Miss Emma. They are all boys here, but I'll keep you safe. You'll have your own place. I'll even get my boys to string up some sheets around your mattress. You'll be needing your privacy, I'm sure." He smiled. "And you'll get your privacy here, I promise you that."

He walked away, looking over his shoulder to have Emma follow him. As the two Mason children walked through the garret, a large attic room scattered with mattresses and one or two straw beds, they held hands tightly. Whatever they were walking into, they would walk into it together.

"How about this one? Tidy enough for you?" he asked and pointed down at a narrow mattress that looked a good deal cleaner than all the others. "And we'll put the old sheets up around it here, do you see? It would be like your own little room. I'm sure we can find a cushion or two for you as well."

"I do see, thank you," Emma said, peculiarly grateful for the fact that Mr Griswold had recognised her limp immediately and hadn't judged her for it. He'd simply moved along, deciding how best to make her comfortable in that shabby place. And that lack of judgement went a very long way with Emma. Despite hearing her mother's voice deep in her mind, she decided there and then that she and David would stay.

"What do you think?" Mr Griswold asked, and she knew that he was asking her about more than the sleeping arrangements.

"You really will take care of him? You won't let him get into any trouble?"

"Of course, I'll keep him out of trouble. He's no good to me in the clink, is he? I have a living to make after all. So, is it settled?" He raised his eyebrows at her.

"Yes, Mr Griswold, it's settled."

CHAPTER 18

"So, as I said, there are two ways you can go about successfully picking a pocket," Freddie spoke with pride and authority as he and David walked side-by-side on their way to the market at Blackfriars. "Do you remember what they are?"

"Yes, to be a *shadow* or to *distract*," David said, grinning broadly when Freddie nodded.

"That's right, when you're out on your own, the trick of the trade is stealth. A good thief must do his best to become his mark's shadow. You have to be right up close to them, but they must never know that you're there, do you see? And then you have to be so gentle, so quick and so soft that they barely feel the touch of an intruding pair of fingers before you have their purse in your hand. And you don't run, you never run! Not unless you've been rumbled, and your mark shouts out. Then you run along

140

the alleyways I showed you, you keep twisting and turning, double back, go around the little blocks, anything to put them off running after you."

"I practised all the streets again yesterday. I know all the alleys, Freddie, and I reckon I could get away from anybody if they caught me." David was keen to please.

"But just to see that you don't get caught, that's my point, David. You've got to be a ghost, a real ghost. You've got to be so good at what you're doing that you could walk along at your mark's side for half a mile and they'd never suspect you of being the one who relieved them of their purse. Not that you ever walk along with them for half a mile, you understand that, don't you?"

"Yes, I understand that," David said and laughed.

Blackfriars market was in sight and David felt a mixture of emotions. He was excited about the morning, about what he would learn from Freddie, about how his own skills might improve. He was afraid also, terrified that either he or Freddie would be caught, and everything would be finished. That he would let Emma down. He knew deep inside that he had failed to protect her and it ate away at him. The last thing he wanted to do was fail again. Deep down, much deeper, was the sense of knowing that this was wrong. Their mama had always told them it was. It was her number one rule. Never steal. David fought hard not to think about it, shaking his head and biting his tongue whenever an image of his mother's face came into his mind. He loved her so much and he missed her every day and he knew, without a doubt, that she would be in heaven now with tears in her eyes. He was letting her down, but if he didn't, he'd be letting Emma down.

"Right, now let's get to the *distracting* approach, shall we?" Freddie went on, blissfully unaware of the internal struggle happening inside David's heart. "Now then, this one is a little more complicated because we have to work together. But as complicated as it might seem, it's safer in the beginning, it will bring you into the whole thing gently. Now then, when you're new at it, you're the one who does all the distracting. You play confused, look sweet, and then ask our mark a question. Usually directions is the best thing to ask for, because it normally takes our toff's attention away from their own pockets, do you see? Anyway, you ask for some directions and you keep your eyes on our mark, not on me. You don't look at me, you don't let your eyes stray to me for a moment, because if yours do, theirs will too. Meanwhile, I'll be relieving them of their coins and you, when you've got your directions, start heading off as if you're following them. Then, when you're out of sight of our mark, you double back and you meet me in the alley down the side of the old tavern, right?"

"Yes, all right," David said, feeling his mouth go a little dry with anticipation.

"So, I'll be the ghost today. I'll be the ghost and you'll be the distraction. You'll learn from me by not noticing me, if that makes sense. That's how we'll do things today and we'll see how you get on. Right, shall we?" Freddie looked forward; they were just yards from the Blackfriars market.

"Yes, I'm ready."

David ran over every part of the plan in his mind again and again. When the time came, he didn't want to make a mistake of any kind. He didn't want Freddie to think he was stupid, and he certainly didn't want to be in trouble with Mr Griswold. He was glad he'd found somewhere for his sister to be safe, but he still didn't like Mr Griswold very much. There was something a bit frightening about him, even with the posh speak he tried to do. Perhaps that was what made him more frightening; the voice didn't go with the rest of him. Whatever it was, David knew he wouldn't let him down lightly. There was something about him which made David wonder how well the man would deal with incompetence.

And so, David did everything that Freddie had told him to do. He concentrated hard; he did everything in his power to look like the innocent little angel his mother had always told him he was. He asked for directions, he didn't take his eyes from his mark's face, not once. He never saw Freddie approach the mark once, he just did exactly as he had been told. And in just that fashion, the two boys had a most successful day out on the streets. So successful, in fact, that Mr Griswold had been obviously pleased with him when they returned to the garret.

But as Mr Griswold congratulated him, as he patted him on the back and told him what a natural he was, David had never felt lower in all his life. He smiled nonetheless, never once letting Mr Griswold see what he really thought of him. There wasn't a choice, and he silently vowed to himself to continue to work with Freddie for the good of himself and his sister.

CHAPTER 19

It was cold in the garret, but Emma reminded herself that it was certainly not as cold as the alleyway at the side of the baker's shop in Clerkenwell. It was hardly a homely place, but Emma had made herself useful in the three weeks since she and David had arrived. At first, she didn't like the idea of washing sheets and clothes for all the boys who lived there, but she soon realised that her own environment was greatly improved by this cleanliness. The place certainly had begun to smell better.

"Looks like you've nothing left to wash, Miss Emma," Mr Griswold said as he watched her washing David's spare shirt. He was lucky to have such a thing, she realised, when she often had to wash and dry the garments of the other boys whilst they were wrapped in a sheet or a blanket to cover themselves.

"Yes, I think you're right, Mr Griswold," Emma said conversationally, despite the fact that she didn't like the man very much.

She was, of course, grateful not to be sleeping in an alleyway anymore, but she had begun to see through Mr Griswold already. All the boys in his so-called care worked every day out on the streets risking their very liberty as they practiced the arts that Mr Griswold had taught them. She knew they brought in plenty of money between them for she had secretly watched Mr Griswold in the dead of night counting coin after coin after coin. That being the case, could he not afford them some better clothes once in a great while or feed them something more nourishing than gruel and bread? As much as he continually told everybody how much he did for them, Emma was older and wiser than the pack and she could see that Mr Griswold only ever twisted and turned the world to suit himself. He took none of the risks and reaped all the rewards and, like so many other adults before him, he sickened her.

"And you've cleaned this place up a treat too, Miss Emma. I wonder what we used to do without you," he was staring at her a little too intently and Emma felt the hair on the back of her neck stand up. She wanted some reason to be out of there for the day, for it was one of those days in which all the boys were out and there was nobody in the garret but her and Mr Griswold.

"I'm very grateful to have somewhere to live, Mr Griswold. And I was thinking I could perhaps be of some help in providing proper meals for the boys. I mean, they have plenty to eat, Mr Griswold, but perhaps a few vegetables, a little warm stew now and again? I would make it all, of course," she added, not wanting to appear ungrateful.

"A little stew?" he said and closed his eyes for a moment as if imagining it. "I think I'd quite like a nice rich stew. Well, perhaps you should go to the market, Miss Emma," he said and dug into his pocket for some coins which he tipped into her open palm.

"I don't think I need quite so much, Mr Griswold," Emma said, getting ready to hand back at least half of the coins. "I really was only going to get a few potatoes, some carrots, and maybe a rabbit."

"Well, you can give me whatever change there is when you get back," he said, refusing to take the coins.

It unsettled Emma a little, leaving her wondering if this was some sort of a test. He'd put several shillings into her hand, and he was staring at her, his eyes looking directly into hers.

"Yes, all right then," she said and quickly put the coins into her pocket and reached for her mother's old shawl to wrap about her to ward off the cold of a late October day.

"I trust you, Miss Emma. I trust you to come back, my dear," he said in his unsettlingly forced cultured tones. "And I know that you're a smart young woman, one who wouldn't need to be told precisely what happens to people who skip out on me with my money." The sudden change in tone and expression was the last thing she had expected, and it took a moment or two for the full weight of his words to rest upon her.

It was a threat, a very obvious threat. He was letting her know that she was able to leave but that she must come back. She was free to go, but she was something of a prisoner at the same time. She felt suddenly trapped and a little nauseous.

"Yes, of course," she said lightly, trying to give away no hint that she had recognised the threat and been made afraid by it.

It took only a matter of minutes to get to the market in Farringdon, but Emma was exhausted. She had found herself trying to move faster than usual, to get away from Mr Griswold faster.

Emma knew from her few whispered conversations with David that he worked either in Farringdon market or the market at Blackfriars. With every step, she wondered if she would see him in the distance, her innocent, angelic little brother reaching into the pocket of an unsuspecting man or woman. It made her shudder and she silently prayed that he might be in Blackfriars that day.

It felt good to be outside, to be alone, and Emma realised that she hadn't enjoyed such a simple thing since moving into the garret the month before. She had been outside, of course, but only ever with Freddie Quince and David or with Mr Griswold himself. There was always somebody there and, following his unpleasant veiled threat in the garret, Emma began to wonder if she had been carefully watched all along.

Emma closed her eyes and realised that she could quite easily have been back in Clerkenwell. Costermongers shouted over one another, each trying to peddle their wares more successfully than the others. She could smell bread and the earthy scent of potatoes everywhere, as could she smell the horrible sourness of rotting meat. Was this just the smell of poverty? Was it the same smell all over London, all over England?

"Penny a pound of potatoes! Come on, madam, who wouldn't want that many potatoes for just a penny?" A young costermonger was calling out to a well-to-do looking woman who walked past with hardly a glance towards him.

Emma smiled to herself when she saw his cheeky grin; he hadn't expected the woman to buy any potatoes at all, he was just having a little amusement. She studied him for just a moment; he was a very far cry from Spuddy, given that he seemed to still have all his teeth and he was a good deal younger. He wasn't richly dressed, but he was smart, nonetheless, and Emma could tell that he was clean. He wore a white shirt without a tie, the sleeves rolled up to the elbows despite the fact that it was, she thought, such a cold day. He had an old but nicely kept black waistcoat buttoned up over the top of his shirt, and black trousers to match.

Emma realised with a start that she recognised him. This was the young boy she had bumped into a few years ago, before she had started working at the big house, before everything had been ripped from her. He was the young boy she had made eye contact with after his failed pickpocketing attempt. He had clearly found his way out of the life of crime, and was now an honest man.

He wore a flat cap over his dark blonde hair and his large cart was a vision of order. Carrots, turnips, cabbages, all neatly lined up. There were apples distinctly separated from the vegetables and barrels of potatoes at either side of the cart. It looked like just the sort of place to buy what she needed.

However, just as she had been about to make her approach, her eye was drawn to a little boy in the distance as he hastily tossed something into a pile of rotting rubbish in the gutter. As quick as a flash, he threw his little hands into his pockets and she knew, without a doubt, that he had just relieved somebody of their coins. She also knew, without a doubt, that it was David. He looked like a different boy altogether, a much more experienced boy, one who perhaps ought not to be trusted. It broke her heart and made her a little unsteady on her feet.

Not looking where she was going, Emma collided with the barrel of potatoes at the side of the costermonger's cart and knocked them flying. The barrel landed with a heavy thump, although she was relieved to note that it didn't splinter. The potatoes rolled everywhere, and she quickly crouched down to pick up as many as she could.

The costermonger joined her in a heartbeat, lifting the potato barrel back to its upright position and helping her to gather up the strays.

"I'm so sorry, I wasn't looking," Emma said truthfully.

"Don't you go worrying about that, miss," the young man said and smiled at her, his skin smooth and his eyes a mesmerising bright blue. "It's not the end of the world and I reckon the potatoes will survive, don't you?" He began to chuckle.

"Well, if I have spoiled any, I will pay for them," Emma said, truly hoping that she hadn't. She didn't want to return to Mr Griswold without having much to show for her money, after all.

"Nothing of the sort, here, let me get those last few." He held out his hand and helped her to her feet before quickly gathering up the last of the potatoes. "There, see, no harm done."

"You're very kind, thank you. And I do want to buy a few things anyway," she added, returning his bright smile with a shy one of her own. "Just a few potatoes, a handful of carrots, and three turnips should do it," she went on.

"Making a stew, are you?" the young man asked conversationally as he took her battered basket from her and began to load it with the vegetables she had asked for. Emma had been right; no recognition had flashed across his face. She really had fallen from grace. But on the other hand, she couldn't detect any judgement in his tone or looks either.

"Yes, I am," Emma said, and everything suddenly felt very normal. She was just a young woman in the market buying a few bits and pieces to make a hearty meal with. At that moment, there was nothing to suggest the life she was really leading.

"Well, you might want to speak to Arthur a few carts down. He's got a couple of rabbits, only small mind you, but he's selling them off cheap because he wants to finish early today. You just tell him that Nigel sent you and I reckon you might get yourself a good bargain," he touched the brim of his flat cap respectfully.

"I will, thank you. That's very kind of you."

"I haven't seen you around here before, have I?" he went on, reaching out to take her coins and rummaging in his pockets for her change.

"No, I haven't lived here very long." Emma felt a little awkward and shy, but she wasn't entirely sure why she had lied. She didn't know why she didn't mention that they had run into each other a couple of years ago, perhaps because then he would see how low she had become.

"Well, you certainly do pretty the place up if you don't mind my saying," he beamed at her, his teeth so clean and straight.

"I don't mind you saying, but I'm sure you say as much to everybody," Emma said, remembering what it was like to be the girl she had once been and enjoying that little moment of teasing between them. It was flirtatious, yes, but not at all tawdry.

"You've got me all wrong, miss," he said, still grinning. "Well, I hope to see you again," he went on and reached out to pat her arm.

His movement was so sudden that it startled her and, without anything but pure instinct running through her veins, Emma withdrew her arm sharply and grabbed her basket from the top of the cart. Her heart began to thump, and she backed away a few paces before turning to hurry from the cart. She hadn't moved so quickly for weeks and the fact that she felt so awkward made her panic, for she couldn't easily get away.

However, by the time she had reached the large terraced house, she paused for breath and realised that she had never been in any danger at all. What on earth had made her withdraw like that? What had made her think for a moment that the young man called Nigel would ever think to hurt her in the way that Jairus Cuthbert had done? But of course, she didn't know him, did she? For all his youthful looks, clean appearance, and friendly smile, Nigel could have been anyone or anything. He could have been the same monster that Cuthbert had been.

CHAPTER 20

"That brother of yours is doing well, Miss Emma. I reckon he is going to be a great asset to me as the festive season begins. Oh, I do like Christmas, Miss Emma. The toffs always carry a little bit extra money and they're so preoccupied with thoughts of their Christmas dinner that they don't guard it properly. Christmas is indeed a time for giving, isn't it?" he said and laughed heartily.

"I see," Emma said and smiled, using the phrase she commonly employed when she didn't know how to answer. She was still disgusted by what she and David had been reduced to, even though she knew that not a bit of it had been in their control. Nonetheless, she couldn't help but think of her mother and how many times she had told her never to steal. She had been adamant, more determined than any person Emma had ever known.

"Everybody enjoyed that stew you made, Miss Emma. It's a pity there isn't any of it left," Mr Griswold went on and crossed the room to where she was.

Emma had been trying to clean the little garret windows, hoping that removing the filth would allow a little extra light into the place. She was feeling far from energetic, but she had wanted something to do to keep her occupied and away from Mr Griswold. They were, once again, alone in the garret, and with every passing day, Emma felt increasingly uncomfortable in his company. Every day felt so long as she waited for the boys to return with their ill-gotten gains so that she could relax a little.

"It bothers you, doesn't it?" Mr Griswold said, surprising her.

"I beg your pardon?"

"Being here, living this sort of life. It bothers you; I can see it in that prim little face of yours."

"Mr Griswold, I didn't mean to be offensive, really. And I'm very grateful to have somewhere to live. Grateful that my brother doesn't have to sleep in an alleyway." He moved to stand right beside her, and it made her mouth go dry.

"I've got to wondering how it is that a young woman as prim as you ever found herself so, fragmented." Mr Griswold said and began to chuckle. "I mean, you hardly seem like the sort to drive a man to wrath."

"I didn't do anything, Mr Griswold," Emma said sharply; she wouldn't be humiliated by the man like this. In the beginning, she had thought him to simply accept her as she was without judgement and it was, after all, the thing which had finally made her agree to stay there in the first place.

"I didn't insinuate you did, never thought it either. Some men can be real monsters, can't they?" he said and nodded.

Emma could hardly work out if he was mocking her or being understanding.

"You'll be safe here; don't you be worrying about anything."

"I see," Emma said, and suddenly wanted to be out of the garret. She suddenly felt anything other than safe. The same feeling she had gotten around Jairus Cuthbert had permeated into the air around Mr Griswold.

"You're still very beautiful, considering everything you've been through Emma." Mr Griswold said. "A man could be very happy with you."

"I was thinking I might go to the market again, Mr Griswold. I did well for just a few coins last time, didn't I? And I think the boys will be healthier, even sharper, for eating good meals. I wonder if I could go out to the market again now and get some more vegetables, maybe even another little rabbit if the man there has them going cheaply again?" She was talking fast and even she could hear the panic in her voice.

It was clear that Mr Griswold heard it too, for he laughed in a most mocking way. Her instinct to dislike him in the very beginning had been right, and his occasional redeeming features of not judging and providing them with a roof did not make up for it. He was a man so used to using others, taking what he wanted, the stolen money he took from the boys at the end of every day, or maybe even a helpless woman for a wife.

"Here, take this," he said and once again put an overly generous amount of coins in her hand. Was it another test? Did he want to know if she would run now that she had an idea of what he expected of her?

"Thank you, Mr Griswold," Emma said and reached for her mother's old shawl.

It was another bright and cold day as Emma hurried along the Farringdon market. She hoped that David wouldn't be there today, that she wouldn't have to witness him so skilfully stealing from others. She knew she would have enough to contend with in seeing the costermonger, Nigel, again. Something about the way Mr Griswold had just treated her made her want to apologise to Nigel, to explain her own behaviour. But perhaps he would be so offended that he wouldn't smile at her again as he had done; he wouldn't laugh or take her battered little basket from her as he filled it with vegetables.

"Good morning, Miss." It was Nigel himself, already looking over at her before she was within yards of his cart. "Another cold one, isn't it?" he said brightly and she realised that he was somehow trying to make amends for the other day.

But he hadn't done anything, had he? He hadn't done anything other than be kind to her, friendly towards her. And here he was trying to find some way to apologise for something he hadn't done when men like Jairus Cuthbert and Mr Griswold walked the earth doing just as they pleased and never, ever said they were sorry. She suddenly felt very shabby indeed.

"Good morning, Mr...?" she said and realised that he had only introduced himself as *Nigel*.

"Nigel. Nigel Harker," he said and seemed relieved that she would even speak to him.

"I'm Emma Mason," she said and shyly held out her hand.

"I'm pleased to meet you, Emma Mason," Nigel said and smiled at her, careful not to hold onto her hand for too long.

"Nigel, I just wanted to say I was sorry for the other day."

"Don't worry, they're only potatoes, they don't have feelings," he said, diverting her even though she was certain he knew exactly what she was talking about.

"I wasn't talking about the potatoes, Nigel, I was talking about you. And I'm certain that *you* have feelings, even if your potatoes don't," Emma said and felt suddenly a little tearful. This was a nightmare, was she really going to cry? "I shouldn't have walked away from you the way I did, it was rude. I didn't mean to, it's just that I'm afraid I don't always know how to trust people anymore." She blinked furiously; she really was about to cry.

"You don't have to explain yourself to me, Emma. And you don't have to trust me either, but I wish you would. It's not easy being new to the neighbourhood and I reckon I'd much rather be a friend to you than somebody you try to avoid." Although he was still smiling, it wasn't the bright and appealing grin that seemed to be his custom, but something more serious, more affecting.

"I think I'd quite like a friend. I don't really have any friends," she said and finally had to give in and hastily sweep the back of her hand across her eyes.

"Don't upset yourself. You don't have to explain anymore, I understand. And look, you do have a friend now, don't you?"

"Yes, I do. Thank you," she said and looked down at her empty basket.

"Do you want the same as before?" he asked, his more jovial smile returning as he took the basket from her hands.

"Yes, please." She smiled and looked two carts down to where the man called Arthur seemed to have another string of rabbits. "Do you know if the rabbits are still being sold cheaply?"

"I expect so," Nigel said with a deep and pleasant laugh. "For Arthur is always in a hurry to get out of here and get down to the tavern. Generally, any time after ten o'clock in the morning and you'll get his rabbits for next to nothing."

"That's good to know," Emma said and began to feel steadier. It was nice to have a simple conversation with a clean and decent man.

She peered about the market, wondering if little David really might be there somewhere. But as her eyes swept about the place, she caught sight of Mr Griswold on the very edge of the market standing at the corner of a large tenement building. He was watching her, and even when she turned her attention away from him, she could still feel him. Knowing that he was there now, Emma realised she had stood at the cart a little too long. It was time for her to make her excuses and leave.

"Thank you," she said, handing Nigel the coins and waiting for the change as she lifted her basket. "Well, I must hurry. I need to get a rabbit and I'll be expected back very soon," she said, hoping that he didn't want more explanation than that. The look in his eyes was enough to tell her that he understood she wasn't entirely free in this world. If only everybody was as perceptive as the bright young costermonger.

"Try to come back again, even if it's only to beat up my potatoes," he said and once again gave her that gentle, understanding smile.

"I will," she said and hurried away.

CHAPTER 21

It had become her custom now to visit the market every other day. Within just a couple of weeks, the boys seemed healthier and sharper and Mr Griswold certainly made no complaints about her determination to provide warming, nourishing meals for them all. She was certain that he followed her every day, and still he handed her far too many coins each trip, safe in the knowledge that even if she wanted to run, she wouldn't get away from him; he would be there watching her, after all.

She went to Nigel's stall each time, spending just a few minutes with him, getting to know him little by little. She knew he was alone in the world, that he only had himself to look out for, although she hadn't yet discovered what had become of his family. Of course, in the poverty-ridden streets of London, any one of a hundred diseases could have spirited them away with ease.

"Ah, here comes my favourite customer," Nigel said brightly as she approached his cart.

"Good morning, Nigel," she said and smiled at him, savouring his fresh good looks and his cleanliness, so rare in her world. "I'm just after my usual, if you have it."

"I always make sure I've got enough potatoes, carrots, and turnips for you every other day, Emma. I just wish that you'd buy half as much so that you can come every day," he lifted his flat cap from his head for a moment and ran his hand through his thick dark blonde hair. It was a subconscious gesture that was so appealing. As always, he had his brilliant white shirt sleeves rolled to the elbows and his neat, black waistcoat fastened around him. He was a tall young man, rather upright, and Emma could quite easily imagine him in much finer clothes, one of the well-to-do gentlemen who unwittingly wandered through the market only to be relieved of their purses by speedy and skilful little boys.

"I wish I could come every day, but I don't think I'd be able to," she said, her eyes darting sideways, subconsciously searching for Mr Griswold. She had never again seen him as brazenly as she had seen him the first time, but she knew he was there somewhere.

"Is that man following you?" Nigel asked, surprising her, still speaking with a smile as if to throw any watching eyes off the scent.

"What man?" Emma asked, swallowing hard and determined not to look around and let Mr Griswold know that she knew he was there.

"Griswold," he said, surprising her even more.

"You know who he is?" Emma said, looking down at the ground.

"I know who he is and what he is. He's an unpleasant man, right enough. But you didn't answer my question, Emma. Is he following you?"

"Yes, he is. He's always following me, but I try not to let him know I've seen him."

"Why is he following you?"

"Because I live with him. I mean my brother and me; he gives us shelter in his garret."

"Knowing him as I do, nothing comes for nothing. I take it he has your brother working the markets, so to speak?" He looked at her without judgement, only the deepest of concern, and while she was perturbed to have him realise her circumstances, the sight of concern in the eyes of another, *genuine* concern, was something of a comfort.

"Well, you know what he is. I want you to know that my brother and I were raised properly, Nigel. It's just that things happened in our lives… things that neither one of us could control. My brother is only ten years old, but he does know right from wrong. We just don't have a choice, that's all."

"I know, I understand. I've been in your position, Emma, and Griswold was there hovering about me, trying to take me under his wing. But I knew what it meant, and I backed away from him. I knew what he would have me do and I wanted to make an honest living." He shrugged and Emma felt suddenly under attack.

"That is an easy thing to do, Mr Harker, when your life hasn't fallen apart all around you." she said sharply and his eyes widened.

"I chose my words badly, Emma, I certainly didn't mean to judge you. And the truth is that I was very lucky at a time in my life when everything else had gone wrong. An old friend of my father gave me just enough money to buy this cart and my first load of goods to sell. If he hadn't done that, you and I would be side-by-side in that garret. I know I was given a lucky chance; I know what I owe."

"Sorry, I didn't mean to snap. I should have known better than to think you were judging me."

"I'm just glad to be *Nigel* again. Nobody ever calls me Mr Harker," he said and laughed, making a show of carefully loading her basket with vegetables. "What happened to you?"

"It was only my brother, me, and my mother. My father disappeared suddenly nearly seven years ago now, and we've never seen him since. We used to live quite nicely. Not well, you understand, but we weren't at the very bottom. Anyway, things went from bad to worse after my father left and we ended up living in a tenement in Clerkenwell. But a few months ago, my mother died of scarlet fever and I lost my position working for Mr and Mrs Hastings in Russell Square. David and I very quickly became homeless after that and spent a night on the street before David got in with one of the boys here in Farringdon. We didn't have a choice, Nigel." She decided to leave out the part where she had been attacked by the old landlord and thrown out of the building when she was falsely accused of a multitude of sins she didn't commit.

"And what are you going to do in the future?" he asked, but she began to feel a little restless; Griswold was out there somewhere watching her, she knew it.

"Sorry, I don't think I have time to tell you. Even if I did know what I was going to do next, I think I have to leave now," she said and looked over her shoulder briefly.

"All right, but don't forget to see Arthur for a rabbit," he said with a smile. "And don't forget to come back here again the day after tomorrow. I'll be waiting for you."

Emma nodded, peering into his bright blue eyes for just a moment before thanking him and hurrying away.

CHAPTER 22

Over the next few weeks, Emma got to know Nigel bit by bit. Knowing they had only a few minutes each time they met, their conversations had become quite intimate and confidential, no time was wasted on simple pleasantries.

It made her feel better that at least one person in the world knew she wasn't happy about her place in Mr Griswold's house. Knew that she wouldn't have chosen her life there out of anything other than an absolute necessity. Nigel felt like a friend, just as he had claimed to want to be, and Emma found herself thinking about him more and more.

He was a handsome young man and one who had a solid place in the world. He certainly wasn't wealthy, but he earned a good, clean living and she admired him for it. He had been able to pull himself out of the squalor she had first seen him in when he was younger, and now he was a fine and honest man. She also admired the way he didn't assume himself to be better on account of it. He recognised good fortune when it came his way and he had the good grace to be openly grateful for it.

"I don't see him anywhere. I don't think he's following you today," Nigel said to her before even saying *good morning*.

"I don't think he's followed me for a few days now. I think it's too cold for him out here," Emma said with a disdainful look. It was true, she was certain he had kept to the garret lately instead of sneaking along behind her. When she returned after her trips to the market, he looked warm and comfortable, not shivering as he often did when he had followed her. Well, if cold weather was the only thing which would bring her a slice of freedom, then Emma hoped the spring would never come.

"Well, that's something, at least, especially if it means I get a few extra minutes with you," Nigel said and took off his cap.

Emma looked up at him, studying him as he ran his hand through his hair, a habit of his which was already becoming familiar to her. How was it possible she had made a friend and got to know him so well in such short bursts?

She liked him so much and realised that her own fear of men had lessened for getting to know him better. Not all men, of course, but she was now able to contemplate the idea that not all men were the same; not all men were bad. His handsomeness and nice ways had attracted her in a way she'd never thought she would feel again. Emma felt like she used to, except now she felt that way with a healthy understanding of what the world really could be like.

"That's a nice thing to say, Nigel," she said shyly, wondering if he felt for her what she was beginning to feel for him. Or was this all just her dreaming again? He'd never mentioned her condition, never once enquiring after how she became a cripple. Had he really not noticed? Or had he noticed right away? If he had, she thought it likely he was just being kind to her, friendly. For what young man would want her as she was? A cripple, who everyone judges and stares at.

"I meant it." He began to fill the basket without even asking what she wanted. "Emma, are you safe there in the garret? With Griswold, I mean."

"I think so," she said and shuddered; she knew she wouldn't be safe forever.

"You know what I'm saying, don't you?" he went on and looked awkward, leaving her in no doubt as to what he meant.

"I'm safe now, Nigel. To be honest with you, I've started to live day by day. If I make it from one end to the other without something bad happening, I reckon I've been safe. We never know what's coming, do we?" she said, wanting him to have the truth but not wanting him to feel responsible for her.

"Do you have to stay there? I know men like Griswold, Emma, they can't be trusted."

"I don't want to be there, Nigel, but I don't have a choice. I don't have anywhere else to go, nowhere to run to." The conversation was taking a turn for the miserable, and Emma wished they could talk about something else, something light which would see her through the day somehow.

"Look, maybe I can help. If you let me." Again, he looked awkward.

As Emma was about to wonder exactly how he meant to help her, her eye was drawn to the sight of David about a hundred yards away. She never looked for him in the market anymore, not wanting to see him forced into such immorality just to look after her. But this time there had been something quite noticeable about him, about his actions, and her heart began to pound. He had clearly dipped into the pocket of a well-to-do looking man with a fine coat and a beard. The man had spun around and David had panicked, running.

Emma could see that the man hadn't seen the little boy darting along behind the costermongers' carts and was looking all about him with an air of confusion as he dug his hands into his pockets and looked for the purse that was no longer there.

David was crouched low as he ran, his face pale and his blonde curls flying as he drew nearer and nearer to Nigel Harker's cart. When he reached them, Nigel gripped him and held him fast, David wriggling in his arms and swearing; words she had never heard him say before.

"I reckon you ought to give that man his money back before you get yourself into trouble, little man," Nigel said in a kindly but in an authoritative way. "Unless you want me to call out for the peelers, of course," he went on.

"Nigel, please don't call out," Emma said, shaking from head to foot. "This is David, my brother," she went on in a hiss.

Nigel lessened his grip but still held onto the boy, his eyes fixing on Emma's in deepest apology. David continued to wriggle, to swear, and Emma felt suddenly ashamed.

"David, don't use that language. Don't say words that Mama would never have allowed you to say in her hearing, I beg you," she said, tears streaming down her face.

"You know I have to take this money back to Mr Griswold, Emma. You know if I don't, he'll throw us out, you know that. Make him let me go, make him let me go now," David said, tears running down his panic-stricken little face.

"It's all right, I'm not going to call out. Just you steady on, David, just calm down," Nigel said, speaking to David in an almost fatherly way. "Do you realise how close you were to being caught? That man knew his pocket was picked and you were just lucky he didn't see you running."

"It was just an accident. There was something funny about the man and it made me look at him too much; it made me too interested in him. It won't happen again," David said, appealing to Nigel.

"I'm not suggesting that you need to be better at pickpocketing, boy, but that you need to stop. It doesn't matter how good you are, you'll be caught in the end. And then where will your sister be, eh? All alone in the world, left there in that garret with old Griswold. What do you think will happen to her then?"

"Please don't, Nigel." Emma's tears were flowing although she spoke quietly, determined that nobody around them should realise what was happening. "There isn't anything he can do about it. There isn't anything either of us can do about it."

"Yes, there is," Nigel said, still holding tightly to David as he looked at her earnestly. "You can come and stay with me. My rooms aren't much, but they're clean and decent. And I'm decent, Emma. I'm not a man who'd take advantage and I think you know that."

"But what would people think if I just moved..." she began.

"And what will they think of you living in that garret with Griswold? People are going to think what they're going to think, Emma, it's time to look out for yourself. It's time to make a change, to take advantage of a small piece of good fortune when it comes your way, just like I did when I got this cart. You have to trust me, Emma. You have to trust me or you'll end up stuck with Griswold for the rest of your life,"

Emma knew then that it was right, that it was the only thing to be done. This was the young man, the handsome young man, of her dreams. This was the man who was always going to come into her life and rescue her from the worst that life had to throw at her. She was suddenly so relieved that she began to cry all the more, nodding her head furiously and smiling through her tears.

"I do trust you, Nigel. I trust you more than any person in this world," she said and when he smiled at her, she felt her heart bloom like a rose.

"What's all this? Thinking of skipping out on me, are you?" The sudden appearance of Mr Griswold made her gasp with shock.

"I'm sorry, Mr Griswold. I was bringing your money, I swear I was," David said, the look of fear in his eyes cutting Emma to the very core of her being.

"I know you were, little champion." Griswold gave the boy a garish smile. "It's not your betrayal I'm bothering about,

David, but Miss Emma's here." He turned to look over his shoulder and Emma realised that he was not alone.

Freddie Quince was there, glaring at her with something approaching hatred. How could a boy so subjugated to an evil, selfish adult, not see himself in her? And behind Freddie were four other boys, the older ones, all of them shuffling from foot to foot, their faces so changed. Gone was the look of appreciation that she had seen when she'd set good food down in front of them. It was as if no moments of kindness had passed between them at all as they stood there ready to do their master's bidding.

"They're coming with me, Griswold. You've lost them, and that's that," Nigel said, pushing David behind him.

"You should have come to me when you had the chance, Nigel. Standing out here day after day for the price of a few potatoes?" He gave the most mocking laughter. "You were always a sharp one and you could have earned twice as much with me."

"Earned it, yes, but never spent it. You send these boys out day after day to take all the risks for you as you snatch the money out of their hands and pretend you're doing them a favour. You are the lowest of the low, Griswold, and if you don't release these two this minute, I'll call out for the peelers. I swear I will," Nigel said and stood his ground so bravely that Emma began to fear for his safety.

"Take him down the alley, boys," Griswold said, and gone were the cultured tones, replaced by the rough, angry bark of the London streets. "Take him down there and work him over."

"No!" Emma cried out and was just filling her lungs to scream when Griswold took hold of her, clapping his hand over her mouth.

"There will be no screaming, Miss Emma, and no peelers. I knew you were betraying me behind my back, and I'll tell you this for nothing, girl, you're about to be very sorry for that."

"You leave her alone!" David said and ran to his sister's side, stamping on Griswold's toe before Griswold reached out with his other hand and gripped him.

Griswold was strong, easily holding onto David and Emma without much effort at all. As she struggled, Emma could see Nigel advancing upon the group of boys, knowing that he couldn't escape them now, he had decided to continue to stand his ground, to be brave. He lashed out, landing several decent blows before the boys swarmed around him like flies and he was done for. They pulled him into the alley so quickly and efficiently, and Emma could see, as she looked all around her, that the other costermongers, all busy with their customers and peddling their wares at the tops of their voices, had seen nothing.

Griswold awkwardly carted her and David to the alley so that they might witness the awful beating that Nigel Harker was receiving. He was already down on the ground, his arms covering his head in an attempt to shield himself from the worst of the kicks and punches. With Griswold's hand still over her mouth, Emma's sobs couldn't escape her throat and she felt hot and sick. The boys she had fed, whose clothes she had washed, whose mattresses she had straightened, had become a horrible pack of wolves. They were unrecognisable to her, lost to humanity in that very moment.

"That's enough, boys," Mr Griswold said, and the pack of wolves stood back, all of them breathing hard, their eyes glazed with violence, their knuckles stained with blood.

Nigel lay unconscious on the ground, his face so bruised and bloodied that it was barely recognisable, his limbs lifeless and awkwardly sprawled. Emma stared at him in horror, certain that he was dead, and wriggled to be free, wanting to go to him, to help him. She needed to know that he was alive, but Mr Griswold was already dragging her away.

"Here, take him." Mr Griswold pushed David towards the pack. "We'll get them back to the garret before busybodies start poking their noses in." And with that, Emma was dragged away, trying to turn to look over her shoulder at the lifeless body of Nigel Harker. The lifeless body of the young man who had wanted to save her.

If Nigel died that day, her old dreams would finally die with him.

CHAPTER 23

"There is a part of me that wants to throw you out onto the streets now, Miss Emma. That would certainly teach you a lesson about gratitude, wouldn't it?" Mr Griswold said as he towered over her.

He'd thrown her down onto one of the other boy's mattresses as soon as she and David had been dragged back into the garret. David was struggling, his thin arms held tightly by Freddie and one of the other boys. Emma was in deep shock, certain that she had just witnessed a foul murder, the murder of a young man she had come to care about. Another decent person swallowed up by the ugliness of the London streets.

"We won't stay, Mr Griswold. We will not stay here!" Emma shouted defiantly as she tried to pull herself up. Her attempt was thwarted, however, when Griswold put a foot on her chest and slowly pushed her back down onto the mattress.

Emma felt repulsed, the memory of the last time a hateful man had pushed her suddenly fresh and raw in her mind. She couldn't suffer that again, she wouldn't.

"Ah, but you will." Griswold sneered at her, his cultured tone beginning to return in a ridiculous parody of an educated man. "I mean, you're neither here nor there, not really. Any woman can cook a bit of stew for the men after all, can't she? But this one, this little one," he said, turning to smile at David who looked at him with so much fury that Emma hardly recognised him as her little brother. "Now, he has unlimited potential. He made a mess of it today, and I'll see that he pays for that, but by and large, he's a very fine little pickpocket. Not only that, he's a very fine little pickpocket who owes me, doesn't he? Bed and board don't come cheap, and it certainly don't come for free. You will be out on those streets over Christmas, David, and I expect you to make more money for me than the rest of them put together. And if you don't, you'll be sorry for it. And she'll be sorry for it too." His foot was still on her chest, although he didn't press down hard and wasn't hurting her, he was just keeping her prisoner.

"You leave my sister alone," David said, breaking free of Freddie and the other boy. They didn't try to grab his arms again, they just laughed at him, a tiny little ten-year-old boy foolishly trying to take on the world.

"Leave her alone? After what she's done? No, you've earned your keep to some degree, David, Miss Emma hasn't, has she? She stayed under my roof and kept warm by my fire without contributing a single thing," Griswold kept his eyes on her as he spoke, running his tongue over his lips in a gesture that Emma recognised all too well.

"Well, it's time you did earn your keep, Miss Emma. You'd never be any good as a pickpocket, but a pretty young thing like you can earn her keep in other ways, can't she?" He narrowed his eyes and Emma could almost feel his disgusting desire as if it were a living, breathing thing. "Starting tonight. Yes, you earn your keep. I know a friend who used to be a vicar, he can marry us within the hour, and then you'll keep your wifely duties"

"No!" David said and darted over to the fire, thrusting his little booted foot into the flames and kicking the contents across the room. The flaming wood rolled out across the floor, immediately setting light to the sheets of the nearest mattress. The fire took hold so quickly that the room was immediately thrown into complete disarray.

Griswold took his foot from her and darted across the room trying to stamp out the flames. He began to shout at the other boys to help him and, as always, they did their master's bidding. David, his young face so much less innocent and trusting than it once was, flew to her side, grabbing her hand and pulling her to her feet. With strength she would never have believed, he dragged her through the garret as it began to fill with smoke. Realising this was their one and only chance of escape, Emma held up her skirts with her free hand and ran the best she could. She knew that her limp was slowing her down, and in turn, slowing down her brother who could have been going so much faster.

However, her determination to survive fought to override her feeling of heaviness, of physical awkwardness, and by some miracle she didn't miss a single step as she and David ran down the stairs. Without looking back, they turned on each landing, labouring down flight after flight. All that mattered at that moment was survival, escape from a certain fate if the two of them had stayed. She couldn't think about the fact that they now had nothing, absolutely nothing. Their few meagre possessions were still in the garret, including David's little train, and they had not a penny between them. But it didn't matter, she would rather die than live like that. Nigel had been so brave that it had cost him his life, she was sure of it. If that was what he had been prepared to lose, then she must be prepared to lose it also.

As soon as they hit the cold December air, Emma began to flag. She slowed down, even as David urged her on. Smoke and fear had made her nauseous, and she could feel her stomach starting to heave.

"We can't stop, Emma. We can't stop or they will catch us and you know what he will do to you. I won't let him; I won't let him!" David yelled, almost screaming in fear.

He gripped her hand tighter still and was dragging her along at a great speed. He began to turn her this way and that, darting along one alley, turning sharply into another. This was the very skill that he had been taught day after day and she had never imagined for a moment that he would have needed to use it to save their lives.

The dull ache in her side was now a sharp pain again, but Emma ignored it. The adrenaline helped with that.

When it seemed that they had run for several minutes, Emma realised that she couldn't carry on. David pulled her around one last corner, and she cried out when they collided with a tall man. A tall, well-dressed man. The tall and well-dressed man whose pocket had been picked by David just an hour before.

He reached out and gripped David, holding him tightly. The boy wriggled in his arms, determined to be free. Emma stood there for a moment, her heart pounding, her mouth working as she tried to come up with a reasonable explanation. But the man's pocket had been picked, what explanation could she give him? Instead, she reached out and tried to pry the man's fingers from her brother's arms, looking beseechingly into his face. And then she realised that it was a face she recognised, a face which made her let go of him immediately and stared up at him.

He had a beard, yes, and his hair wasn't as dark as it had once been, but the man she was looking at now was, without a doubt, Benedict Mason. He was her father, the man who had left them nearly seven years before.

"David, just stop struggling, I'm not going to hurt you," Benedict said, and Emma realised immediately that he knew that they were his children.

CHAPTER 24

"David, stop. It's Papa," Emma said, her voice a strangled, emotion-ridden version of itself. "It's our father," she went on, her entire body shaking with shock and relief.

How was it that he was there so suddenly? Of all the places in London, how had her father been in Farringdon, in that very alley, on the very day and at the very moment when they needed him the most? It seemed like a miracle to her and she didn't have the strength or wherewithal to even ask him where he had been these last years. All she knew was that the very thing she had prayed for since she was a girl no older than David was now there in front of her. Her father, her beloved Papa.

"You're my father?" David said, narrowing his eyes and peering up at the man as if he didn't trust him. For all the adults who had lied and behaved appallingly, why should David trust just one more?

"I am your father, David, and I am so, so sorry." Benedict Mason dropped to his knees and wrapped his arms around the boy, holding him tightly to himself. David stood rigid for a moment, not recognising the man and still so terribly afraid in the wake of their most recent ordeal. However, as Emma watched, tears streaming down his face and his shoulders shaking with sobs, David relaxed. He was a little boy in such need of a father, in such need of someone to lean on, to remove the responsibilities which ought never to have been his. He fell against Benedict, sobbing, clinging to the man who was undoubtedly no more than a stranger to him.

"I knew it was you, I had this feeling. When you took my purse and ran, I knew you were my boy."

"You didn't give chase," Emma said, sniffing loudly. "You looked for all the world as if you hadn't seen which way he went."

"I'd already seen peelers wandering the market, Emma, and I didn't want to draw attention to David. I thought to let him go and leave the market, but I had every intention of returning to look for you, which is why I'm here now. I've searched these alleyways looking for you for an hour. God must be smiling on me today, because I had never thought I would find you so quickly." As he spoke, Emma could see the tears shining in her father's eyes.

He looked so different with the beard, his greying temples making him look so much older than he was. He was so changed from the man she remembered, the youthful-looking man with a ready smile and a smooth chin. And even when their lives had been going well, her beloved father had never dressed so fine. He wasn't exactly what others might call a toff, that was certain, but he was not a poor man either. His coat was very fine, and his boots were sturdy and well-made. He was well-to-do if not wealthy, a man of some means. But where had he been? Why had he left them all alone? Emma's heart was struggling with both relief and anger, a curious mixture of emotions she had never felt so strongly.

"This is how we've had to survive since Mama died," Emma said, suddenly feeling a little cold towards the man she loved so well. She saw the look of sadness in his face, but there was no shock. "You knew she died?" Her voice was almost accusing.

"I've known it for a month. I've known it ever since I came back to London. I knew you wouldn't still be in the same place, for my poor Pamela could never have afforded to stay there, but I searched Clerkenwell for you and that was when I discovered that she died of scarlet fever." The first of his tears finally fell. "My poor Pamela, struggling and suffering to keep you safe, all alone for seven years."

"And what now, Papa? Do you finally take back your responsibility, or do you leave us here with thieves and pickpockets? Do you leave us here to be beaten and abused for the profit of others?"

"Emma, my dear girl," he released David and rose to his feet, reaching his arms out for her. But Emma stood still, suddenly not trusting him, not believing that a man who could so easily abandon his children to their fate would do anything for them now. For all the time she had longed for him, still, Emma did not know what his return might mean for her and David.

Before Benedict had a chance to explain, a chance to put his children's minds at rest or otherwise, Emma turned sharply. She'd heard footsteps approaching them from behind in the alleyway and she began to shake once again. There, creeping up on them, was Mr Griswold and Freddie. The other boys walked along behind, the boys who had joined Freddie in the murderous assault on Nigel Harker.

"I hope these two aren't bothering you, sir," Mr Griswold said in a friendly, cultured tone. "They're a little cheeky, I'm afraid, but good children otherwise. Come along, Miss Emma. Come along, David, it's time we were going home," he went on, smiling at Emma in such a way that nobody on earth would have believed him to be the evil, vicious creature he was.

"You think these children are going with you, do you?" Benedict stood up to his full height, his arms by his side, his shoulders back.

"Yes, of course. I am their guardian, sir, and I do my best to look after them. Still, children are children, and they get themselves into all sorts of scrapes. If the boy took anything from you, my dear man, allow me to make amends." Griswold was rooting in the pocket of his trousers and produced a handful of coins.

"David took nothing from me that didn't belong to him already, I can assure you." Benedict said and Emma could see that Mr Griswold looked confused. "And I'm afraid they won't be going with you today, nor any other day. These children are coming with me."

"I can't let that happen, sir," Mr Griswold said, his face contorting, showing the world what he really was. He put his coins back in his pocket and began to rub his hands together. "I am their guardian and they are, as such, my property. You might have taken a liking to them, but you certainly can't have them." He spoke with all the confidence in the world.

"My name is Benedict Mason and I am their father. Emma Mason is my daughter and David Mason is my son and there is not a person in this world who owns them, do you understand me?" Benedict took a step towards Griswold and Emma sucked in her breath.

"Papa, no. They have just killed a man; you must step back." She was shaking, staring at Griswold and silently praying that God would spare their father and not take him as he had taken her mother.

"I am their father and there is no man on earth or devil in hell who will take these children from me and have them live in a den of thieves. Oh yes, I can see you for what you are," Benedict said, still advancing upon Mr Griswold, even as the boys began to gather around him. "For my own son to have picked my pocket in the street, you are running a den. You are running a den and you have these poor boys doing your bidding. Well, you will not add my own children to their ranks, believe me," Benedict said.

Emma felt her heart almost burst with love for him. How could she not have trusted him? How could she not have believed that he would take them now and look after them?

"What proof do I have that they are yours?" Mr Griswold asked, and it was clear that he wasn't about to let them go so easily.

From the other end of the alleyway came the sound of running feet and, before Griswold and his boys had a chance to run, the whole place was swarming with peelers. Benedict took a hold of his children, grasping their hands and holding onto them tightly.

"What the…?" Griswold began and threw Freddie Quince in front of him, distracting the peelers as he turned to run and save himself. But he ran in the opposite direction and immediately collided with a man who gripped him hard, twisting his arm up his back and holding it tightly, painfully. The man pushed him against the wall and held him there until two of the peelers came over and relieved him of his quarry.

"Is that the one? The one who set the boys to beat you?" one of the peelers asked loudly.

"Yes, that's him. He has a garret full of poor boys in one of the terraced buildings here. He forces them out to work every day. He's turned them into animals, he's made them what they are. Let the magistrate know that, would you? Let the magistrate know that these boys didn't have a choice." As the man spoke, Emma stared at him, open-mouthed. He was beaten and bloodied, the flesh around his eyes and cheeks so swollen that he was almost unrecognisable. But that blond hair, that fine waistcoat, that wonderful voice, she would have known it anywhere. It was Nigel Harker.

Her relief that he still lived was so great that Emma's vision began to blur, and she felt herself tumbling through the air, falling into darkness, before letting go of her consciousness altogether.

CHAPTER 25

When Emma came to, it was to find herself in a clean and comfortable bed. A real bed, just like the one she had slept in as a child. Like the one in the days before her father had disappeared.

As her eyes adjusted and the room came into sharper focus, she could see that she was in a very fine place indeed. It was a bedroom, a real bedroom. A separate room all of its own, not a corner of a single space just marked out for sleeping.

"Emma, are you awake? Are you all right?" It was her father sitting next to her in a chair by her bed, his face grey with fatigue and concern.

"I'm all right, Papa. But where's David? Where is he?" she said, scrambling in the beautifully clean sheets as she tried to get out of the bed.

"He's perfectly safe, my dear sweet Emma. He is downstairs in the kitchen with the housekeeper having some bread and butter. Little does he know that she has him lined up for a bath, but I thought it best not to forewarn him," he said with a chuckle.

"A housekeeper? Downstairs? This is a house? A real house? Is it yours?" Emma asked, staring at him in disbelief.

"I expect you're wondering how it is I live so well when my children have suffered so badly?"

"I'm grateful to be here, Papa, and grateful you're here, but yes, that is a question I would dearly like to hear the answer to," Emma said, knowing that she ought to keep quiet, to be silently grateful, to keep her place there in her father's house. But at the same time, she had to know.

"What did your mother tell you when I left?"

Emma shook her head. "Nothing, she would never tell me... at the end she said it wasn't your fault."

He shook his head and his expression was a mixture of sadness and pride. "Your mother never said? She never told you where I went, where I was sent?" he asked again as if to be sure. His face was so familiar to her now, as if they had never been parted.

"She wouldn't speak of it."

"Then it was in kindness to me, Emma. I was in disgrace, but she wouldn't have me seen that way in the eyes of my own children."

"In disgrace for what?"

"For stealing, Emma. It all went wrong you see. I'd had a good job and a blessed life, even if I did work hard. But I couldn't see that at the time. I only saw the men that were above my station, and how they lauded their positions on everyone below them. Instead of thanking God for what he had provided me with, I coveted after other's lifestyles."

He stopped and dropped his head for a moment. She reached out and squeezed his hand.

With a smile he looked up at her. "These supposed great men of business, they don't play by the same rules as everyone else, or rather, they bend the rules every which way. I tried to be like them, I tried my hand at skimming off the top, of pocketing things here and there to further my own cause. But I'm no thief, Emma, I'm not an experienced man in such arts. I was caught almost instantly, and thrust before the magistrate. Things have changed in the last few years, but those long years ago, my act of theft saw me transported to Australia. I never saw my children again, and only the desperate face of my weeping wife as my sentence was handed down. For the last seven years I have turned myself inside out wondering what had become of you all."

"You were sent to Australia?" Emma said, relaxing now, settling back into the soft pillows as she found herself transfixed by her father's story.

"I was sent to Australia. And I felt every one of those thousands of miles, believe me."

"But how is it that you're back here now, Papa? How is it that you live in such a nice house?"

"I was given a second chance in Australia, thank God. It is a very different place from England and my skills as a reasonably well-educated man were quickly seized upon. I worked in a shipping office, learning the trade quickly. The company was not doing so very well when I first arrived, but I worked hard, and I helped turn their fortunes around. The owner of the company was so grateful that he paid me well and gave me a very fine position. More than that though, he brought me to the Lord. I had completely lost my way in the business world here, and my sinfulness was what drew me to thievery. In Australia, I gave my life to the Lord again, and became dedicated to being the righteous man I always should have been. I hated myself for so long, but with the help of God, I have come to finally forgive myself, and I hope that one day you can forgive me too."

Emma's father took a pause to wipe a tear from his eye, before continuing on with his story. "When I finally admitted my plight to my boss, when I told him of the family I loved and missed so much back in England, he gave me the task of setting up a new office in London, an office on the bank of the Thames. That is how I am here now, that is how I am paid well enough to afford such a house as this. As soon as I came back here, the moment I took my first steps on England's soil, I came to look for you."

"Where are we, Papa?" Emma said. "Where is this house?"

"Blackfriars."

"And how did you come to be in Farringdon?"

"I was looking for you. I was looking for you both. My enquiries in Clerkenwell were exhausted. I'd tracked down the tenement where your mother had taken you to live and found Mr and Mrs Appleby," he said, screwing his face up in disgust. "And that was where the trail ran cold. I just kept moving from place to place, searching the markets, hoping I would see you. I believe it is God's good grace which led me to find you on the very day you needed me."

"And I expect Mr and Mrs Appleby took great delight in telling you why they had cast David and me out onto the streets?" Emma said, looking down.

"They gave me their version of things, but I knew it wasn't true. I was furious when I walked away from that place." He said, and she had no doubt at all that Vera Appleby had given him the most appalling version of his daughter that he was ever likely to hear. "But I bumped into the costermonger outside and I asked about you. He was a shabby little fellow, but it was clear to me that he'd cared about you both."

"Spuddy?" Emma questioned, surprised to find she was greatly relieved to hear that he was not in prison. "But how did he manage to escape prison?" Emma said and shook her head. "He's a good man, Papa, and he did something very silly." She felt compelled to explain, not wanting her father to think that she only ever chose low company these days. "He'd had one drink too many and he foolishly tried to pick the pocket of a man related to a magistrate."

"Yes, I discovered that much. But his apology together with the fact that he hadn't actually managed to relieve the man of his purse went in his favour and he escaped with a fine. But that is by the by, Emma; he told me how you'd suffered. He told me about Jairus Cuthbert, a man who was killed in a fight in the tavern. He said that he'd hurt you, that he would have sworn blind that he was the man who had permanently hurt you."

"He did, Papa. Just a week after Mama had died, he dragged me into his room. He knew I didn't have Mama there to protect me anymore and he thought he could do whatever he wanted. And he..." Emma said, crying at the memory of it all.

"I am so sorry I wasn't here for you, Emma. You're my responsibility, both of you, and I will work the rest of my days trying to make up for all the horrible things, all the losses, all the pain. This is your home now. This will always be your home. We are a family again, and I will never, ever do anything to ruin it." Tears were rolling down his cheeks and Emma reached out to wipe them away with her thumb.

Benedict pulled his daughter into his arms and held her tightly, both of them crying, both of them held tightly in the grip of their own emotions.

"I wish Mama was here," Emma said miserably.

"So do I, my sweet girl. Your mother was the love of my life," he said and sounded so heartbroken that Emma knew it to be true. "I'm sure she's looking down on us from Heaven smiling."

At that moment, the bedroom door creaked and they both looked to see David wandering in, slightly awkward.

"You have milk on your face and crumbs all over your chest, son," Benedict said and laughed, quickly dashing away his tears and seeming grateful for a moment's respite from his own tumultuous emotions.

"Yes, my tummy hurts too," David said, rubbing his belly as he advanced into the room. He looked young again, innocent, his messy blond curls and his big blue eyes returning him to the angel he had once been.

"Then I expect you've eaten more bread-and-butter than you should have," Benedict said with an indulgent laugh.

"Mr... I mean, *Papa*," David began tentatively, looking at Emma for confirmation that the man really was his father. "That woman downstairs is trying to put me into a bath," he said, his young voice scandalised in a way which made his father and sister laugh.

"There are worse things in this world than being clean, son," Benedict Mason said in a voice dripping with love.

"Are there?" David looked unsure.

"David, be a good boy. Don't have Papa think that I haven't kept you as clean as I could these last few months," Emma said, grinning and reaching her arms out for him.

David hurried across the room and clambered onto the bed, letting his sister wrap her arms around him and laying his head against her chest.

"We are a family again now, aren't we?" Emma said, looking at her father.

"We most certainly are, Emma. You will never know how sorry I am. You will never know how much I missed you both," he said, and wrapped his arms around the both of them. "And I promise you, we'll have a Christmas to remember."

CHAPTER 26

Emma was getting used to the fine terraced house in Blackfriars bit by bit. In her wildest dreams, she'd never imagined living in such a place. She'd never even imagined living as well as the family had once lived seven years before, so this was a dream well and truly surpassed.

By some miracle, David had been utterly returned to the sweet, innocent child he'd been before their lives had spun out of control. He looked more like an angel than ever with his blond curls clean and fresh and his neat little trousers, shoes, and shirt. And Emma felt like a princess in the pretty dress her father had had made for her.

Mr Griswold had been convicted in court, there were plenty of market regulars who were more than glad to witness against him, and even some of the boys who had been under his reign spoke out against him. Freddie

Quince never did though, and was taken away with Mr Griswold. David had cried for his friend, who was too far gone to save now. He and Emma kept Freddie in their prayers each night from then on out.

"The house looks wonderful, Papa," Emma said, wandering into the sitting room where her father sat reading the newspaper. "I should have made the decorations," she went on, looking at the beautiful holly garlands and knowing she had not the first idea how to make something so wonderful.

"I want this Christmas to be the best, Emma. I don't want you to have to lift a finger. You've worked hard enough in your life already and it's time you rested."

"Where's David? I can't find him anywhere," Emma said, not panicking this time, confident that wherever her brother was, he was safe.

"He's gone to the market with Mrs Hollister," her father began. "Clerkenwell market, I hasten to add."

"Goodness, doesn't Mrs Hollister mind going all that way?" She glanced out the window to see snow falling and a light covering on the ground. It made everything look special, made it look like Christmas and she knew David would be delighted. Running and chasing in the snow was a young boy's dream. Perhaps Mrs Hollister would enjoy seeing him so happy, despite the cold and treacherous conditions.

"Not really, she's taken a shine to David. And anyway, he was determined to see Spuddy. He has a scarf and some gloves to give him for Christmas and he wouldn't settle until I let him go." Benedict laughed. "He's a good boy, he has a tender heart."

"Spuddy's a character, but he was good to us. You know, he used to call me the Duchess?" Emma said and laughed. "I suppose he thought I was a bit hoity-toity at times, funny really, since we had absolutely nothing."

"You might have had nothing, Emma, but you were never rough. Your mother raised you well." His eyes looked sad as they always did when he talked of the wife he had lost. "And David seems to have come out of the whole thing quite unscathed. I have a lot to be grateful for."

Emma smiled and closed her eyes, letting her head loll sideways until it rested on her father's shoulder. She thought of Spuddy, and she thought of David's excited little face when he saw his old friend again. How she wished she could ask her father if she could go and find Nigel. He'd risked his life to protect her and David but she realised that, as far as her father was concerned, he was simply a goodhearted costermonger who had stepped in to help them.

She hadn't yet spoken to her father about Nigel, about what he had meant to her in the weeks that she had spent living in the garret. Emma had wanted to tell him how

Nigel had almost rescued them in the last minute, offering to throw open the door to his home and let them in.

Emma wished with all her heart that she could look upon his handsome face just once more. Those bright blue eyes and that dark blond hair; the way he took his flat cap off now and again and ran his hands through that thick blond mane.

Life had taken a turn for the better, Emma didn't need rescuing anymore. But she realised then that her attraction to Nigel had truly had nothing to do with her salvation. He was a good and kind man, a clever and humorous man, and a brave and true man. She knew she had begun to fall in love with him in those little slices of time that they'd shared every other day whilst she lived in the garret. But on the day that he had so selflessly put himself in harm's way, Emma knew that she loved him. She truly loved him.

She hadn't said anything though. She was terrified of what Nigel would think of her now. He had been such a help to her, and in return, she had caused him to get beaten half to death. Would he even want to look upon her face ever again?

Emma was just about to tell her father all about Nigel, when the sound of the door swinging opened interrupted their comfortable silence.

"We're home!" David said, flying into the room in his neat woollen jacket and flat cap. "Spuddy said that I looked like a proper little gent. Oh, yes, and he asked after you, *Duchess*," he went on, his accent a little roughened as it always was when he'd spent time with Spuddy.

"Don't you start that Duchess business with me, cheeky chops!" Emma said, laughing as she reached out to playfully tug one of his pristine blond curls.

"Duchess, Duchess, Duchess, Duchess," David said, full of happy excitement as he twirled about the room teasing his sister. Benedict, looked on, smiling contentedly, his eyes shining again with tears. He was an emotional man who wore his heart on his sleeve and Emma felt her own heart squeezed to think of how he'd managed thousands of miles away without them for so long. It must have torn him in two.

"Come on, you," Mrs Hollister said, breathlessly bursting into the sitting room with her arms folded across her chest. "We don't wear our hats and coats in the house, do we?" She scowled at David, but Emma could see the care in her expression; he really had won the housekeeper's heart.

"All right, all right," David said, grinning at her. "And can I have a mince pie, Mrs Hollister? You said I could."

"Yes, but just one. They're for Christmas day as well you know." She ruffled his hair and smiled indulgently.

"But that's only the day after tomorrow. It's almost Christmas day now, Mrs Hollister."

"It's nothing like Christmas Day, you cheeky boy. Now come on, hat and coat and then you can come down into the kitchen and have a mince pie."

Emma watched her brother being led away by Mrs Hollister, hand-in-hand as they disappeared from the room. He had a mother again; she could see it. As much as she had tried to be a mother to him, their circumstances had prevented her from taking that role completely. He'd had to look after her in the end, but now he had that special relationship, that most important relationship to a child.

"I'm so glad you found us, Papa," Emma said, sniffing and holding back joyful tears.

"And so am I, my sweet girl. So am I."

On Christmas morning, Emma had stood in the little church at her father's side, determined to ignore the glances of several pinched faced women in the congregation. They didn't know her circumstances, they didn't know what she had suffered. Well, let them be who they were in a house of God and have *Him* judge them as they judged her. She felt free from all of that, knowing she had an unconditional love in not only her earthly father, but her Heavenly Father too.

They returned to the house, greeted by the wonderful smell of a slowly roasting turkey. Mrs Hollister began to bustle like a woman with a mission, throwing off her good coat and replacing it with her thick apron as she checked the turkey and the potatoes, noisily thanking God that nothing had burned in her absence.

Emma set the table, still greatly impressed that the family would even sit down at a real table to eat. She set out the polished knives and forks neatly, taking the greatest care, determined to do her own bit for that most wonderful of Christmas days. When it was done, she went back into the sitting room to join her father and brother.

"Come, open your gifts. Poor David has been waiting for you so excited, wiggling like a worm. Go on then, open them up, son," Benedict ruffled his son's hair and watched as David excitedly tore open the brown paper.

The best of his gifts was a new wooden train, crafted in such a way that Emma knew, without a doubt, that their father had made it for him, just as he had done the last one. David immediately rubbed at his eyes. A little boy had never looked more thrilled, and Emma surreptitiously dabbed at her own eyes.

"It's just like my old one, Papa," David said, grinning at his father before rushing across the room to throw his arms around him.

"And open yours, Emma," Benedict said, pointing at two parcels on the rug beneath the Christmas tree.

Gently opening the first parcel, Emma found the most beautiful dress contained within. She stood up, holding it against her. It was such a pretty material, pale blue and pink, so strangely familiar to her.

"Oh, Papa, thank you," she said, smiling up at him, dabbing her cheeks with a handkerchief.

Her father simply smiled, and nodded to the other parcel.

Emma opened the second parcel and realised why it was she had recognised the fabric of the dress. She looked down in her hands at the pale blue and pink bonnet, the bonnet which matched the dress to perfection. It was *her* bonnet, the one she had looked at so long ago as she stood at her mother's side peering into the shop window at everything they couldn't have. It was the bonnet she imagined wearing when she was rescued by her handsome hero. It was the bonnet she had hoped never to see again when her world came crashing down around her.

"Oh, Papa," she said, bittersweet tears flooding her eyes, making her temporarily blind. "How did you know?"

"David told me," he said, kissing the top of his son's head as he sat in his lap clutching tightly onto his wooden train. "He's sharper than you think," Benedict went on, laughing.

"He most certainly is," Emma said, smiling at her beloved brother.

"And there's something else," Benedict grinned at David who grinned back. "He told me about something else that would make you happy on Christmas Day. I suppose I should have given you a little bit of warning, but I wanted you to be surprised."

"Surprised by what, Papa?" Emma asked, hastily blowing her nose.

"We have a guest for Christmas dinner," her father said, extricating himself from his son and making his way to the door of the sitting room. He opened it and peered out, clearing his throat and greeting whoever it was standing silently in the corridor. "Come on in, my dear fellow."

Emma, still kneeling on the floor by the Christmas tree, looked up to see none other than Nigel Harker walking into the room. He looked more handsome than ever, so fine in a dark grey wool suit, his shirt pristine, his waistcoat beautifully neat. His blonde hair was tamed, there was no sign of the flat cap he wore every day in the market. Her mouth fell open in surprise and Nigel laughed, giving her that broad grin she knew so well.

"Merry Christmas, Emma," he said, walking over to where she was and reaching down a hand to her. She took his hand and allowed him to help her to her feet, standing before him with so many emotions swirling in her chest that she couldn't count them.

"Merry Christmas, Nigel," she said and then fell into his arms, weeping tears of joy.

It really had been a Christmas Day to remember and, by the end of it, Emma was utterly exhausted. They had all sat around the table for the longest time, Mrs Hollister, amusing and formidable, holding court and making them all laugh. Her father certainly couldn't have picked a better addition to their little household.

As day turned into night, Nigel declared that it was time for him to go home. When Emma said she would show him to the door, neither her father nor Mrs Hollister made any objections.

"I had a wonderful day, Emma," Nigel said, putting on his fine overcoat and hat as he stood at the door. "I'm so glad to see you again."

"I wanted to find you, Nigel, but if I'm honest, I didn't know what you would say. They almost killed you, and I wouldn't have blamed you if you never wanted to set eyes on me again."

"I think you know me well enough to know that I understood none of it to be your fault. I know we got to know each other in a strange sort of way, but I don't think I ever got to know anybody so well in all my life."

"I've missed you so much. And I want to tell you how I feel about you but even now I'm terrified. I mean, look at me; you've never said anything, but surely you must have seen," she glanced down ashamedly at her leg.

"None of that matters to me, it never did. I knew that first day that you were special, not just because you're the most beautiful girl I ever set eyes on."

He paused for a moment and Emma stared up at him, her heart pounding and so full of joy and excitement.

"You were so full of dignity and poise," he said. "Strong and fragile all in the same breath. I knew right from the start that you were in trouble. But you always made it look easy, as if you could cope with anything in the world. How could I not have fallen in love with you? And I did fall in love with you. I fell in love with you on day one." He slid his arms around her cautiously, as if he expected her to struggle, to push him away.

She didn't, nothing had ever felt so right in her entire life. No touch could have been further away from the awful attack that Jairus Cuthbert had subjected her to. Emma wrapped her arms around his neck and held tightly to him, so grateful that life had finally come right in the end. She had everything she could have hoped for, and all that was missing was her beloved mother.

"I love you, Nigel," she said in a whisper.

"And I love you, Emma. You're the reason I am where I am today."

Emma pulled out of the embrace in confusion. "What do you mean?"

Nigel smiled. "I knew I recognised you when we first spoke in the market, I just couldn't quite place the memory, but now I can. You watched me the day I got caught trying to pick a man's pocket. That day I almost succumbed to Mr Griswold's temptations, but something distracted me, or should I say, someone."

"Me?"

Nigel nodded. "The most beautiful girl I had ever seen. And since my first foray into pickpocketing had been such a disaster, I swore to never steal again."

Emma looked down. "I feel a lot less beautiful now than I did then…"

Gently, Nigel lifted Emma's head up so her eyes met his. "I still think you are the most divine person I have ever set my eyes on. I need to talk to your father but… Emma Mason, will you marry me?"

Emma felt her eyes spring wide open. This wonderful man would ask her such a question, even after knowing all she had been through. Everything about him was so so wonderful. "Yes," she whispered. "Yes, yes, YES."

"That is the best Christmas present ever. Let me kiss you once before I go. If you don't hurry back to the sitting room, Mrs Hollister will be out here with a broom." He laughed and Emma did too.

She leaned her head back and looked up at him, so thrilled when he finally kissed her. It was the most thrilling moment of her life, a moment she knew that she would never forget.

"Well, I'd better be going," he said, releasing her.

"All right, but you will come back. You will, won't you?"

"I'll never leave you, Emma." Nigel said, and she knew he meant it.

EPILOGUE

"If things keep going as they're going, we'll soon be moving out of your father's house, Emma," Nigel said, joining her at the window of their bedroom. "I never thought I'd have so much money saved up!"

Emma had been looking down into the street, feeling sleepy and a little distracted. She was happy, that much was true, in fact, she had never been happier. Her beautiful baby daughter, Noelle, had fallen asleep on the bed, a chubby little child of thirteen months, exhausted from a night without sleep. The last of her little teeth were coming and it had given the poor child something to cry about night after night.

"I'm not so sure that Papa will be pleased to hear it. He still likes to have David and me around him all the time, you know that," Emma said, leaning against her husband as he put his arms around her. "I think you'll need to give him a little time."

"He can have all the time he needs, my darling wife. I owe him so much, so much that I'll never be able to thank him enough. And of course, we'll stay here for as long as you want." He kissed the top of her head.

They really did owe her father so much. But as her father told it, he owed Nigel *everything*. Nigel had been prepared to rescue his children, prepared to lay down his life in defence of them. As far as Benedict Mason was concerned, it was a debt that *he* could never repay in full. And so it was that he had given his new son-in-law a very good position at the London branch of the Australian shipping company. He'd recognised immediately how bright Nigel was, how good he was at reading and writing, and how easily he would pick up the workings of his new trade.

Nigel had accepted immediately, knowing full well that when God hands you a blessing, it is best you to take it with both hands. As the shipping company's fortunes continued to soar, so did those of the Masons and the Harkers. David was in school, a bright boy of almost twelve who enjoyed every lesson, already determined to follow his beloved father into the shipping industry.

And although Emma could still see the sadness in her father's eyes from time to time, nobody could have been more thrilled than her to realise that that fine man was falling bit by bit in love with the robust and strident housekeeper, Mrs Hollister. She was already a mother to David and Emma knew that, in no time at all, she would be a wife to her father. She could never have imagined life turning out so well, all its jagged little pieces finally falling into place, creating something whole and wonderful.

On the day that she had given birth to their first child, Nigel had not left her side. Despite Mrs Hollister's stern misgivings, Nigel had held onto Emma's hand from that first squeal of pain to the very moment her baby daughter was placed into her arms. Emma would always be grateful that he'd been there. He held Noelle, soothed her, adored her, and loved her with all his heart.

"Anyway, when this next baby comes, I think I'm going to be very glad of Mrs Hollister," Emma said and grinned at Nigel. "Noelle is hard enough work. Goodness knows how I'll manage when this one comes along." she said, patting her barely swollen belly.

"Let's hope it will take Noelle's mind off her teeth," Nigel said and chuckled.

"Oh, for goodness sake, by the time this one comes along, Noelle will have all the teeth she needs," Emma said and laughed loudly; how her handsome young husband made her laugh every day.

Looking back, she could hardly imagine that the pain and suffering she had experienced had been real at all. At times it felt sharp, real, but when she was in the arms of her loving husband, such experiences seemed a million miles away. She knew she had so much to thank Nigel for. He had dissolved her fear of men, the idea that they were all dreadful, evil beings. He'd soothed her pain of being a cripple, and helped her to live again.

He'd helped her to trust, and to trust so much that she was more in love than she could ever have imagined being in all her life. He was the handsome man who had rescued her, the man she had always dreamed of. He was whole and real and beautiful, and she would thank God every day for the rest of her life for everything. Emma knew that every steppingstone of her life had been a steppingstone that was leading her towards him. Every awful thing had been another point on the map of her life, the only route which could ever have led her into his arms.

And that was what life was, as far as she was concerned. A series of points on a map. But the route between those points was something that a person decided for themselves. A person could either give in or keep walking forward and she knew now, as she looked back, that her young self had never given in. Even when she had wanted to, even when she thought she had, Emma had never truly given in.

"I love you, Nigel. I'll love you forever."

"And I'll love you forever, Emma. My wife; my beautiful *wife*."

THANK YOU FOR CHOOSING A PUREREAD BOOK!

We hope you enjoyed the story, and as a way to thank you for choosing PureRead we'd like to send you this free book, and other fun reader rewards...

Click here for your free copy of Whitechapel Waif
PureRead.com/victorian

Thanks again for reading.
See you soon!

HAVE YOU READ?

CHRISTMAS DOORSTEP ORPHAN

Now that you have read 'The Orphan Pickpocket's Christmas'
why not continue with another seasonal Victorian Romance?

The courage and faith of Emma's story is similar to that of a brave young girl bearing the same name in the precious PureRead tale called *Christmas Doorstep Orphan*

This story begins on a frosty Christmas Day. An unexpected arrival shakes the opulent world of the Leigh-Donner family in Belgravia. A mysterious note claims the abandoned child is their kin, but they're reluctant to embrace her as their own...

What will happen to little baby Emma?

You'll not be able to stop turning the pages of this warmhearted historical yuletide saga! 🩶

PS: Prepare to shed a few happy tears!

Here for your enjoyment are the first chapters of the Doorstep Orphan's story...

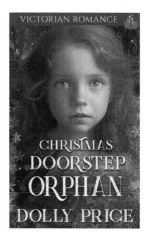

"Good morning, Colonel, and you, too, Madam. May I wish you both a very merry Christmas." The butler entered the breakfast room with a covered platter of hot sausages, bacon, eggs, smoked fish, and toast to serve the colonel and his lady personally, which he always did on special occasions.

"And we wish you the same, Perkins," replied his mistress. Her husband took the cover off the platter, and the delicious aroma of Christmas breakfast filled the room.

"There was a snowfall during the night," Mrs. Leigh-Donner said.

"It has begun again, Madam." Perkins looked toward the window, and their eyes followed his, just in time to see a carriage halt outside amid the whirling snowflakes.

"There is somebody out today," the colonel said. "It's too early to be Charlotte and the children. The neighbours have visitors, I expect."

The doorbell rang, startling them. Who could be at their door on Christmas morning?

"Excuse me," Perkins said, setting the platter down and making for the door.

"Very odd," remarked Colonel Leigh-Donner.

They heard voices in animated debate in the hallway.

Perkins burst into the room, rather quickly for his usual gravitas.

"It is a policeman, Colonel, to see you and Mrs. Leigh-Donner, and he bears a -" he stopped, for the constable was upon his heels and had entered the room. In his arms was a small child covered in a blanket, a woolly cap about the head. The child was asleep.

There was amazement.

"What, is he injured? Lay him on the easy chair, and we will fetch a doctor." Mrs. Leigh-Donner assumed that there had been an accident outside their door.

"No, it is not that." Perkins was red-faced and very agitated. "The constable says there is a note come with her."

Trembling, he thrust a piece of paper into the colonel's hands. There, he read, in bold capital letters, the following words.

MY NAME IS EMMA. I WAS BORN ON 1ST JULY 1859 IN A COUNTRY FAR AWAY. PLEASE TAKE ME TO MY PATERNAL GRANDPARENTS AT 11 ELIZABETH STREET, BELGRAVIA.

"Emma! My own name!" Mrs. Leigh-Donner fainted.

"She was found last night at Victoria Station in the ladies waiting room," said the constable. "She spent the night at the police station, wrapped up as warm as they could make 'er. Where shall I set the child?" He was getting impatient, for he wished to be rid of his burden, and he was forming the idea that the couple at this address had no wish to be acquainted with the child. It was a long way to a workhouse, and he had no wish to go there in a snowfall.

The housekeeper, Mrs. Breen, appeared then, and having been shown the note by Mr. Perkins, took the child from the constable, who made a hurried departure.

Assistance was found for her mistress, who was recovering. The colonel was stricken dumb.

"I shall take the child downstairs and give her milk," said Mrs. Breen. "What a shock!"

~

Mrs. Leigh-Donner was able to sip some hot coffee and managed a slice of toast and a little poached egg. The colonel ate a hearty breakfast. He always said that eating helped him to think, and not even a shock like this would cause him to neglect his Christmas breakfast.

"Grandparents indeed! She cannot be our family," Emma said flatly. "Our boys are good boys."

The colonel said nothing. He had been in the army a long time and knew that plenty of young men sowed their wild oats while their mothers at home thought them saints.

They had two living sons, and neither was in England. Wesley was in India, a bachelor, he planned to marry when he returned on his next leave. He would hardly risk his chances with Lady Margaret Winston by sending home evidence of an indiscretion.

Lewis was in Italy on a European tour. They were in regular contact with Lewis; he was destined for Oxford and the Church. It could not be Lewis.

A silence ensued as there was one name left.

"Could it be...could it possibly be Cyril?" Emma asked in a very, very quiet voice.

The breakfast room was hung with doubt and possibility, hope and despair.

"No, it cannot be Cyril," her husband replied flatly and somewhat derisively.

"But, suppose he is alive?"

Cyril, the oldest son, was a captain in the British Army and had been missing, presumed dead, in the Crimea five years before.

"How could he be alive and not come home? How could he be alive and father a child in adultery? Have sense, Emma. Eat something."

"Charlotte will not like it," she admitted then, "if he is alive, and did not come home to her, and neglected her and the children all this time, and perhaps stayed in the Crimea and had a second family."

"It is a preposterous thought! Put it out of your head!"

"But he may be alive, just think! What if my Cyril is alive all this time! They never confirmed he was dead. They never found the bodies."

"He is dead, as are Corporals Brown and Enright."

Captain Cyril Leigh-Donner had led Corporals Richard Brown and James Enright up a steep hill on a scouting mission. An hour after they had left, the camp had heard shots from the hill. They had never been seen or heard of again in spite of extensive searches. They knew all three. Brown had been a young footman and Enright the coachman in the Leigh-Donner household. It had been a dreadful blow when they had heard the devastating news. The house had gone into a long mourning. The parents of the other two men lived in Spitalfields and Whitechapel, only a few miles from each other. Mrs. Leigh-Donner had visited them and given them consolation and help.

Mrs. Leigh-Donner rang the bell and ordered the child to be brought up to them. When she arrived, she was taken in her arms while she scrutinised her keenly.

"If you're looking for a resemblance, all infants look the same," her husband said, annoyed.

"She is getting past the infant stage, when resemblances begin to form. Do you not think that her eyes could look like ours, a little?"

"It's your imagination, Emma. Do not even begin to dream that Cyril is alive. This is not Cyril's child. He did not have fair hair."

She rumpled the thick fair tresses.

"Hair colour often changes!"

The child was awake and Emma, feeling restless, walked with her about the room. They came to a cabinet upon which was a group of photographs.

"Papa," sang the little one, pointing straight at a head and shoulders photo of Cyril.

"She is Cyril's! She is!" Mrs. Leigh-Donner became very excited. The colonel sighed in frustration and gulped back his coffee. If his son was alive and well somewhere, and in his wits, he was not only an adulterer, but a deserter and a disgrace. Better to believe him dead!

"It's Christmas morning, and Charlotte and the children will be here soon. Is all well with the kitchen preparations? Get your wits about you, Mrs. Leigh-Donner!" His black bushy eyebrows, the terror of his men, were drawn together in a frown.

"Yes, of course."

"Send the child down to the servants and we shall see what is to be done with her later on."

Mrs. Leigh-Donner pulled the bell again.

"Is my Cyril alive?" she asked herself, caressing her son's photograph. There must be some strange explanation for this, an explanation in which her son would come out blameless of course. He had lost his memory. That was it! He had married and regained his memory. But her ideas petered out in the improbability of it all.

The housekeeper and butler said nothing downstairs about the note, and the staff were astounded at the sudden appearance of a child in their midst. She was placed in the care of the under housemaid while the servants prepared for their guests, Mrs. Cyril Leigh-Donner and her three children and their nursemaid.

They arrived at two o'clock full of Christmas merriment and gifts for their grandparents and sat down to a table laden with roast turkey stuffed with pork, baked ham dripping with syrup, golden roast potatoes, brussels sprouts, carrots, and lashings of gravy, with wine for the adults and lemonade for the children. But Charlotte noticed something wrong. Her parents-in-law were always a little sad about Cyril at Christmas, but always made the effort for the sake of the children. Today, even the jovial Grandfather was drawn and silent.

After sending the children out to play in the back garden after the Christmas pudding had been served, she asked them what the matter was. They had no choice but to inform her of the morning's happenings and to show her the note.

"It can't be Cyril," she said, her voice tremulous.

"Why not?" her mother-in-law asked sharply.

"He is dead."

"Quite so, Charlotte," Colonel Leigh-Donner said.

Charlotte's hands were shaking; she put her coffee cup back on the saucer with a giveaway tinkle. She had fallen out of love with Cyril a few years after they married, and he with her. They had been very young, she seventeen, he twenty. He had not been a bad man, but authoritarian like his father, and she had begun to suffer under his tight control and domineering way. While she never wished him dead, after seven years she would be free to remarry if he did not return. She was in love again, and Mr.

Marshall was patiently waiting until she could be declared free.

"It cannot be Cyril," she said flatly.

"She pointed to his portrait and said 'Papa,'" Mrs. Leigh-Donner said firmly. There was a very uncomfortable silence.

"What will you do with her?" Charlotte asked.

"We do not know," her father-in-law said.

"It must be a hoax," Charlotte went on. "It is well known you have a son missing, presumed dead, and someone wants a good place for their illegitimate, nobody child. Is there no way to find out for certain?"

"It appears there is not," Mrs. Leigh-Donner said. "Her clothes are not of the best quality but decent, and she is clean. She has been taken care of. She has a few words, but they are unintelligible."

After dinner, Charlotte went downstairs to the servant's hall to see the child for herself. She was sleeping on a small couch, two chairs drawn up close to it to prevent her from falling off. She gazed at her and satisfied herself that she looked nothing like Cyril's other children.

"She looks common," was her verdict. "It's a hoax, a deception, to get her a good life. She has a cunning parent who would risk that, but it is so cruel to pretend that Cyril is alive, when he is not! And why do my in-laws not think of their other two sons? It would be a good trick indeed, for either of them, to point a finger at Cyril's being alive, when they know he is not."

When her mother-in-law asked her to take the baby home with her because she had a nursery, she refused, and left that evening in a very bad temper. Unlike the first Christmas, this Christmas had been ruined by the arrival of a small child...

What will happen to this unwanted babe? How will the bairn's future unfold? Continue reading this unforgettable story in Christmas Doorstep Orphan, the new Christmas novel by Dolly Price.

Continue Reading Christmas Doorstep Orphan on Amazon

LOVE VICTORIAN CHRISTMAS SAGA ROMANCE?

If you enjoyed this story why not continue straight away with other books in our PureRead Victorian Christmas Romance library?

Read them all...

Churchyard Orphan

Orphan Christmas Miracle

Workhouse Girl's Christmas Dream

The Winter Widow's Daughter

The Match Girl & The Lost Boy's Christmas Hope

The Christmas Convent Child

The Orphan Girl's Winter Secret

Rag And Bone Winter Hope

Isadora's Christmas Plight

~

PLUS THESE BRAND NEW CHRISTMAS TALES
FROM OUR BESTSELLING VICTORIAN
ROMANCE AUTHORS

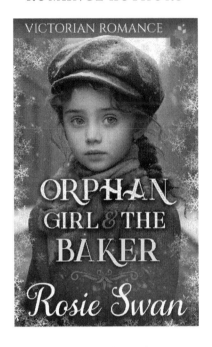

Read Orphan Girl & The Baker on Amazon

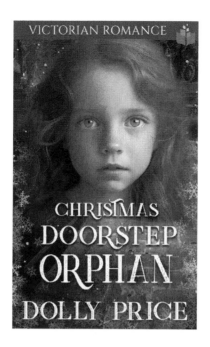

Read Christmas Doorstep Orphan on Amazon

OUR GIFT TO YOU

AS A WAY TO SAY THANK YOU WE WOULD LOVE TO SEND YOU THIS BEAUTIFUL STORY FREE OF CHARGE.

Click here for your free copy of Whitechapel Waif

PureRead.com/victorian

At PureRead we publish books you can trust. Great tales without smut or swearing, but with all of the mystery and romance you expect from a great story.

Be the first to know when we release new books, take part in our fun competitions, and get surprise free books in your inbox by signing up to our free VIP Reader list.

As a welcome gift you'll receive the story of the Whitechapel Waif straight to your inbox...

Click here for your free copy of Whitechapel Waif

PureRead.com/victorian

Printed in Great Britain
by Amazon

30488682R00135